A LONG DAY'S EVENING

A LONG DAY'S EVENING

Bilge Karasu

Translated from the Turkish
by Aron Aji and Fred Stark

City Lights Books • San Francisco

Originally published in Turkish as
Uzun Sürmüş Bir Günün Akşamı © 1991 by Metis Yayinlari, Istanbul

Publication of this work was supported by TEDA, a program of
Turkey's Ministry of Culture and Tourism.
Aron Aji's translation was supported by an NEA Literature
Fellowship.

Library of Congress Cataloging-in-Publication Data
Karasu, Bilge.
  [Uzun sürmüs bir günün aksami. English]
  A long day's evening / Bilge Karasu ; translated from Turkish by
Aron Aji and Fred Stark.
    p. cm.
  ISBN 978-0-87286-591-4
  1. Monks—Byzantine Empire—Fiction. 2. Faith—Fiction. 3.
Istanbul (Turkey)—History—To 1453—Fiction. I. Aji, Aron, 1960–
II. Stark, Fred. III. Title.

PL248.K33U9813 2012
894'.3533—dc23

                         2012025687

City Lights Books are published at the City Lights Bookstore,
261 Columbus Avenue, San Francisco, CA 94133.
www.citylights.com

To Müge Gürsoy Sökmen
—A.A.

CONTENTS

BY WAY OF A PREFACE

A *Long Day's Evening* is one of those rare works that al-
ter a nation's literature; with it, Bilge Karasu introduced
a remarkable dose of freedom and experimentalism into
Turkish fiction. Nothing quite like it had been written before in Turkish, and much of the noteworthy fiction published since bears traces of it. A reader in six languages and
translator from several, Karasu was richly cosmopolitan,
achieving a deft synthesis between international and local
narrative modes. Turkey's Nobel Laureate Orhan Pamuk
is often cast among the likes of Calvino, Rushdie, Eco, and
rightfully so; yet Pamuk's postmodern playfulness, poly-
phonic narratives, and genre-crossing also have much in
common with the work of Karasu, arguably the first Turkish postmodernist.

Originally published in 1971, *A Long Day's Evening* contains three narratives held together by several
thematic dualities — among them, faith/creed, truth/
dogma, image/signification, freedom/loyalty, liberation/
oppression. The book is made of two conspicuously un-
equal parts. The first part has two sections ("Island" and
"Hill") narrated from the point of view of two Byzantine
monks, Andronikos and Ioakim, each of whom endures a
wrenching crisis of faith during the period of iconoclasm,
when their mode of worship is forbidden by decree. The
common plot elements, the relationship between the two

9

monks, and the overlapping time frames cast these two stories as a single coherent narrative, told from two perspectives. The second part ("The Mulberry Trees") is quite different, a brief, self-contained story set against the more familiar backdrop of twentieth-century intellectual history. Suggestively autobiographical, the story focuses on an author writing in the 1960s. That decade had begun with a military coup in Turkey, an event that was seen then and for some years afterward as a liberation, because it toppled a government considered oppressive by many people, especially students. The paradox of liberation by force — a scenario that has been repeated in Turkey at least twice since — inevitably sends us back to the Byzantine Emperor Leo III's terror, ostensibly aimed at freeing Christians from idol worship and affirming true faith.

Because the political tenor of the third story is considerably more somber, Turkish scholars have at times asserted that "Island" and "Hill" ought to be read separately, and some have even expressed regret that Karasu chose to include "The Mulberry Trees" in *A Long Day's Evening*. Yet it is certainly possible — I want to say, necessary — to approach the book in its totality. Each of Karasu's major works contains narratives that appear to have been created in overlapping time frames across several books. As such, the book proper presents itself as a studiously constructed and reconstructed artifice that renders its invention process integral to its scope. Moreover, the three narratives in *A Long Day's Evening* unfold, quite beautifully, in a sonata form: Andronikos and Ioakim are the "movements" through which the major themes are developed, and the last fifteen pages serve as a striking — and unsettling — coda that transforms the historical novel into a fascinating act of self-interrogation through invented others.

A Long Day's Evening can be read as Karasu's companion to the crisis-of-faith literature penned by many authors whom he admired: Dostoevsky (*The Brothers Karamazov*), Kafka (*The Castle*), Yourcenar (*The Abyss* and *Memoirs of Hadrian*), Camus (*The Fall*), Céline (*Journey to the End of the Night,*) Mishima (*Patriotism*), and O'Neill (*A Long Day's Journey into Night*) — the book's title in Turkish is nearly identical to those by O'Neill and Céline. The meaning of the names Karasu gives his monks, Andronikos (man victorious) and Ioakim (God's chosen), inevitably alludes to the conflict between humanism and dogma central to all these works.

◆

The emergence of a literary text means that, first, its language has been made to express that text. . . . Literature is . . . the memory of language. I am not saying the memory of individuals, it's the memory of language.

— Bilge Karasu

For Karasu, a dynamic correspondence exists between language and the literary text, as language shapes and takes shape inside the literary artifice. Meaning materializes in and through language. Things, ideas, emotions, experienced in inchoate form in ordinary lives, germinate, ripen and find their most authentic reality in and through language, which itself is consciously developed in order to express this reality. Karasu's language — complete with deep structures, metaphoric resonance, inner rhythms and sounds — effects a mode of expression to correspond as closely as possible to one's mode of thinking and meaning-making. His unconventional form and syntax (fragments, extended run-ons, indented clauses, dispersed paragraphs, and so on) are intended to capture the moods, rhythms, and pace of an acutely self-conscious imagination in search of self-understanding. The stories in *A Long Day's Evening* begin with the plainest conversational language, and gradually acquire an almost operatic quality as the themes interweave and the language mirrors their complexity. To find correct English correspondences requires not only grasping the idiosyncrasies of Karasu's language but also somehow *inhabiting* the existential space created simultaneously by that language.

One example: In the original, the common conjunction *ve* (*and*) is absent. On one level, the omission has to do with the Arabic root of the word, and Karasu's rejection of vocabulary borrowed from other languages. However, this gesture carries an existential significance as well: Particularly in the first two stories, the Byzantine world being described is overwhelmed by imperial edicts that separate, that divide individuals from each other, from their kinship groups, their beliefs, their homeland; the crisis of faith effected by the prohibition against icons ultimately divides the very self, alienating the person from his values, faith, thoughts. In this light, the absence of *ve* reinforces the severe isolation of individuals. To re-create this existential dimension, I chose not to use *and* throughout "Island" and "Hill," which also helped to heighten the introverted, meditative character of the narratives.

◆

It is true that the twentieth century, saddled with the ruins of the nineteenth century, has become an era much debated by people who have found, exposed, interrogated the wrongs of the past, who have attempted to acknowledge, to imagine, to construe new ways to acknowledge, those wrongs; but regrettably, it appears to have failed to do, all the way into its last years, anything other than exhibit over and over examples of the bloodiest, the most ruthless, the most senseless treatment of the other. Technological progress, even in the areas where it seems the most useful, can become another name for oppressing the other, inflicting on him unimaginable agonies.

In these pieces, I am trying to understand. I am as much us as the other, we are, we all are, us as much as the other. I am trying to understand us, what separates us from the other. That's all.

— Bilge Karasu, Preface to *Other Writings*

✦

Loyalty, personal identity, otherness, belonging, freedom, authenticity — these are also deeply relevant to Karasu's personal history, as he was born to an Eastern Orthodox mother and a Jewish father. In his lifetime, Karasu refused to describe himself as anything other than a citizen of the modern Turkish Republic, and insisted on being known by his pen name. However, it is very difficult to experience the world of *A Long Day's Evening* — one steeped in questions of faith and otherness — and to resist acknowledging Bilge Karasu's own liminality.

✦

A Long Day's Evening was the first book I was given to translate. Seventeen years and many other translations later — including Karasu's *Death in Troy* and *The Garden of Departed Cats* — this particular evening has now arrived. I am indebted to Müge Gürsoy Sökmen, Karasu's Turkish publisher, for her stubborn faith and encouragement. This project was generously supported by a National Endowment for the Arts Translation Fellowship. I also thank my colleagues at St. Ambrose University, Davenport, Iowa, and the students and faculty in the University of Iowa's MFA in Translation program for their continued support. A most sincere thanks to Elaine Katzenberger of City Lights, not only for her wonderful edits and insights but also for her continued interest in Turkish literature. And I gratefully acknowledge Fred Stark, a good friend of Karasu, and a superb translator, who agreed to share the pages of this book with me — he is the translator of the book's third section. Not having known Karasu in his lifetime has been one of my enduring regrets; yet his books have certainly carried me into many beautiful friendships. This book is dedicated to all of them.

— *Aron Aji*

A LONG DAY'S EVENING

Translated by Aron Aji

ISLAND

He turns to look ahead. He must be getting close to the island, since the dark imposing mass of its rocky peak has grown more distinct in the advancing dawn. His exhausted arms pull the oars with the numbed ease of a body that has grown indifferent to thought or will. He can hardly hear sounds. The oars plunge into the water, withdraw, plunge again; the sea tears open, yielding to the boat, mends itself in the morning calm.

He turns to look again. The island, getting larger as he approaches, appears to shrink in the glow of the sun rising from behind it. The first rays are about to touch the surface of the sea. A soft breeze makes Andronikos shiver, carrying the whisper, the scent of pine needles from the island. It has been a very long time since he experienced a new scent, different from everyday scents or even last night's smell of fish, seaweed, salt. . . . Still, Andronikos has no time to enjoy such distractions, though his soul craves them. He knows it shouldn't but can't say why. An indistinct grin settles on his lips, which would have been considered a smile of sorts in the monastery, in Byzantium. Once upon a time, when he used to belong to a community, more precisely, until yesterday — when he finally realized that he had made himself believe all along, that he had deceived himself into thinking that he believed he belonged to a community. No, it wasn't yesterday but the day before. Morning is breaking; yesterday is already more than a day ago.

From now on, he'll have time. Abundant time. To die, to live, to experience new things. . . . In fact, so much time that it will have no intrinsic meaning or value. How best to use this time? He ought to do something. Perhaps create something. Yet to create, to find the strength to create something. . . .

Andronikos laughs. He still can't resist the seduction of such nonsense, such absurd reasoning. This deceptive, good for nothing, impotent. . . .

No, not impotent. Such reasoning shouldn't even be called impotent. He shouldn't forget that he accepted impotence from the start. So that he could use the word "love" often, freely, with dizzying abandon, until he made believers of others, made them nauseous with his play on words, until he convinced himself, too, that love is the mainmast of the universe, he accepted impotence from the start. . . .

He releases the oars to keep his palms from bleeding too much. How often he has had to release them since the start of his journey, he's lost count. (Why even count? He should stop counting at least for now.) He plunges his hands into the water. He can hardly feel his battered palms, as though they're not his, except for their pain, a sharp, hissing pain — like water spilled in scalding oil.

This, too, will pass, he thinks, this exertion at the oars. Soon he'll have to carry stones. For the next few days or just hours perhaps. He doesn't know.

Yet to create something, one must first believe. Above all else, believe. . . .

He is caught in the snare of impotence, worse still, in the void of his circuitous thinking. But what if he is? What would be the harm, given that being caught or being free have become equally meaningless now? Even if he were willing to relive the past two days, even if he were to descend again into the swamp to start over, Andronikos would still fall prey to his reasoning. . . . Impotent or not.

He is thirty-three years old. The same age as the peasant who at the end of his life was nailed to a cross on a hill in Palestine, unaware that he had changed the world. . . .

But Andronikos shouldn't be thinking of him at all. So much has happened, so much is happening still, it seems, on account of the crucified one. No use in deception. Events are happening not because of the one on the cross, but because of the strife among his believers on both sides who equally believe that they are his true believers.

What's the use of assigning blame? Today, of all days. . . .

He settles back to his impotence.

Now the sun ushers in a soft breeze, combing the water. He can see the sea floor glistening under the deep, resonant shade of green — like glass, like fresh fruit, like ice. Exhausted, Andronikos doesn't want to turn his head to see that the island is saturated with the ever more intense sunlight. He knows that it is, he doesn't want to look. Although the air is getting warmer, he feels a slight chill, the residue of last night's cold that is only beginning to subside with the rising sun. Andronikos is pleased with himself. It's good to take note of real, tangible details, small sensations like these that keep one distracted. He shouldn't fall asleep yet.

The water turns dark suddenly, assuming a deeper shade of green with streaks of black, yellow. Andronikos pulls in the oars. He's not a sailor; one could almost say that he learned to use the oars during the passage last night. But when the water turns dark, one pulls the oars in — a bit of common knowledge that requires no prior experience or reasoning.

The undulant weeds spread out like flower stems, rising to the surface. Now the rocks emerge. It's time to look behind to figure out where to bring the boat ashore.

He steers slowly, cautiously, in order to avoid grounding the boat. He's not familiar with the rest of the shoreline, but here, on the island's west side, the shore is quite rocky. What matters is that he has arrived. The water swells almost imperceptibly. He stands up; the boat wobbles. There's a narrow clearing among the rocks — visible under the water — leading to a gravel bank. He'll try to follow the clearing.

Darkness lifts as the island's once looming shadow recedes with the rising sun. Close to its edge, the water gives way to gravel. From beneath the boat comes a rasping sound, at first faint, then harsher, like wood being forced against its grain. Andronikos is unsure whether he should use the oars since he doesn't want to damage the boat; he decides it would be safer to get into the water instead.

He lifts his robe, puts one foot in the water. It's cold. He laughs, amused by his sense of decorum, then lets his robe fall in the water. Carefully, he manages to bring his other foot over the edge without tilting the boat too much. Then he plunges in. It's deeper than he estimated, deeper than it looked. The seabed feels slippery; seeking flat rocks with his toes, he tries to move forward step by cautious step, pulling the boat along. The water feels warmer now that his legs have gotten used to it. His robe that first swirled around his waist then clung to his knees now clings to his calves.

He emerges from the water, hauling the boat, its bottom grating the rough sea floor. The stones hurt his feet. These are large, round, flat stones; even so, walking on them is not easy. . . . Andronikos keeps pulling the boat away from the water, far enough that the waves won't sweep it against the large rocks. The safest would be to move it up to the higher end of the shore. He pulls, pushes, drags, struggling to avoid damaging the boat. Now he gathers up his provisions, his shoes, his rope, his knife, the hammer he bought two days ago in the market, his chisel, the ax. Then the round of cheese, the flour sack, his jar of honey. . . .

Staring at the not-insignificant pile of his belongings, he laughs again. Will he find water? He must. He places the oars inside the boat, which he thinks will be safe here. If it rains, the rocks rising high above the boat will shelter it, channel the rainwater away from it. The elevated pebble shore will bar the tides or threatening waves. Pirates? If they come, they come: Andronikos can do nothing against them. Best to leave the boat here, he decides.

He puts everything he's just piled on the ground into in his sack. Putting on his shoes, he wraps the laces around his ankles once, then ties them. He'll leave the sack behind. He can come back for it later. First, he has to find a path, perhaps tracks, water. . . .

He tucks the sack under the boat, just in case. But he may need the knife, the rope. He pulls the sack out, unties it; taking out his knife, the rope, he pushes the sack back under the boat. The knife's handle has a ring through which he passes the rope; he ties the rope around his waist. His hands are free. For a very long time, his hands haven't felt as free, as liberated. . . .

When he wasn't holding the cross, he was holding the icons, the censer or the hands of the blind, the cripples, the children, their mouths, their lips, candles, bibles, rosaries. . . . The oars, sleepless, invincible oars.

He shakes himself. It's not time to fall asleep. He scans his surroundings. The rocks are too steep, yet he must climb them, open a path for himself. He can't remain on the shore. He has to climb the hill. Whatever way he can find to do it.

Above the hill the sky is luminous. He decides to turn right, since to his left the rocks looming over the boat appear discouraging. Even if he starts climbing, he won't be able to get very far, since he can't see even a single crack to grip or use as a foothold. To his right, perhaps, there is a way. . . .

He walks the narrow arc of the pebbled shore, alongside the tall cliff, until he can go no further when he finds himself standing at the mouth of an inlet. Wedged between tall rocks, the water heaves toward what appears to be a hole. His eyes fixed on this hole, Andronikos notes that it isn't entirely submerged. He removes his shoes, lays them high on a rock, throws himself into the water. His feet hurt as if burned; each time he moves them, a wisp of blood mixes with the water. What he did was foolish. He should have noticed the jagged lime deposits, the sharp shells covering the rocks. He's more careful now, but it's already too late. . . . The salt water soothes his cuts. He moves cautiously. The rocky sea floor begins to narrow. He should untie the rope around his waist, disrobe, dive in naked to bathe his whole body. He lays his robe to dry on the shore, securing it with a stone. . . .

He crawls into the water carefully, to avoid hurting his knees, palms, belly. Soon he reaches the mouth of the hole. He has to decide whether to go in. He'll try it.

He listens. Each time the water heaves through the opening, he hears reverberations in the distance. Maybe the hole leads to a cave. He should try going in. When he was a child, in the years before he entered the monastery, he used to go outside the city walls to swim with other neighborhood children. He had learned how to swim well, how to dive. Now he's about to do something he hasn't done for years.

Taking a deep breath, he plunges through the opening. Seaweed brushes against his belly, his thighs. There are no shells. As the opening narrows, he has to stretch his arms over his head in order to pass through. But he can't. He's out of breath. He shouldn't drown. He has to go back. Back, farther back, faster.... Until he's surrounded by light. He thrusts his head above the water. Feeling dizzy, he takes another deep breath, dives again. This time, he stretches his arms farther. Gripping the rocks, he pulls his body through the narrow opening. He knows he won't survive if the surface is rough. But it isn't. His hands come out of the water, then his head emerges. He stands up. Inside an immense cave.

The entire space is drenched in translucent green. In the center of the cave is a pool, its water the deepest shade of aquamarine, its bottom coated with slick, soft, immaculate white stones. Sitting on the edge, Andronikos scans the surroundings. One could live here for a while. But the difficulty of access makes the idea uninviting. Besides, he is neither running away nor afraid. Why should he stay here?

The water was warmer. Andronikos begins to feel cold. Perhaps because he hasn't slept yet. He has to stay awake for a while longer. He's not sure where the light is coming from. A certain amount is seeping through the opening, but the actual source of this breathtaking translucent green has to be some place else. Perhaps there's another opening. Another mouth, another inlet, another....

He gets back into the water, takes a deep breath, then dives. His arms moving more freely this time, he passes through the opening. Crawling briefly, he comes out of the water. The sun has risen. The air feels warm. He wipes the water off his naked body with his hands. He picks up his robe from the rock. It has dried. Good. Very good. He feels invigorated. I should come down to swim every morning, he thinks, then catches himself: In order to come down, one must first climb up....

He scans the tall rocks surrounding this end of the pebbled shore. In the past, the nobles of the city used to come to this island for excursions. The regal, splendid boats probably didn't moor on this side of the island, even though it's closest to the city. Maybe today he should rest. Tomorrow he can row to the other side to search for an old trail to climb the hill. Whatever it takes, he ought to climb the hill. From the top, he'll be able to see the entire island, perhaps spot a building once used by the courtiers who entertained on the island. Even among ruins, it's conceivable that he'll find a habitable corner. Or bricks or tiles he can use. Andronikos isn't sure. Others may have found shelter in those ruins, or fishermen might have settled there. Still, not too many people would take the trouble to climb the hill. Andronikos decides he'll try.

He puts on his shoes. Right above the cave, he sees a flat rock that will receive his first step.

The sun has risen further. His back is burning. He must reach the pine grove, whatever it takes. His exhausted body won't endure the heat.

One could sleep under the pines, even eat a morsel of bread. Sometime last night, he had torn off a piece of the loaf, chewed it for a long while. He hasn't put anything in his mouth since then.

Once he's standing on the rock, the climb seems more manageable. Right above, he spots another flat rock like the one under his feet. Each time his hands try to grip the surface, rock fragments crumble down. It's impossible to hold onto the soil. Maybe if he scratched it with his knife? The soil slowly yielding to the blade's tip, a notch begins to emerge. He needs to dig deeper before he can close his hand on it. His knees begin to sting. If he can find another notch, he'll pull himself up. Some more exertion. . . . He grabs an exposed root. The rest gets easier. Andronikos is amazed at himself when he reaches the next flat rock. He wasn't sure that he would be able to.

From here on, the slope is less steep; he's able to reach the top of the cliff by crawling on his knees along a path covered with dried pine needles. One can't be too careful with them. Soon he's standing among the trees. They look like black candles grown soft with heat, bent, twisted. A grove of giant candles with broad, sprawling flames, dark green. . . . He keeps walking. The ground is almost level now but still slippery. If he loses his footing, he'll grab onto tree trunks or roots. He has enough bread in his pocket to curb his hunger, at least for a while. The piece left over from last night. Later, he'll have to descend for provisions. The thought of descending discourages him. But he'll deal with it later; for now, he needs to think of nothing else but climbing. That is, he needs to find a way, or make a path, to continue climbing.

A light breeze under the trees. The faint noise of the grove humming lightly in the breeze. Pine scent. But unlike that of a few trees scattered around a garden, it's the sharp, overpowering redolence of pines stretching farther than his gaze can contain, covering all the space that is not the sea. Unable to withstand it, he lowers his body, leans his back against a tree. The breeze isn't cool but hot, fragrant. Yet he does feel a certain coolness on his skin. Never forget the sea, he says to himself. He hears his voice — faint, reluctant. He needs to get used to hearing it. Even alone, he needs to get used to being heard. He needs to remember, to revive everything that the monastery called upon him to forget. Even if he has to live like those monks who endured the pious ordeal of solitude on this island, three hundred, four hundred years ago. Their faith never wavered, whether they lived on the hilltop, in the wilderness or the desert. At least that's what people believed.

Was it so in reality? Or was it the belief itself that satisfied the ones who chose to stay behind in the villages or in the city, those whose lives depended on the company of others because they couldn't be weaned from the sedative of multitudes? No one knew. In the monastery, some of the hermits were transformed into legends. The power of their faith was believed to have conquered mountains, fierce beasts, the devil. . . . Still, there ought to have been among them more than a few who, bewildered by loneliness, mistook dreams for reality, eagerly accepted their own voice, their own shadow, as signs of other, immaterial beings. How else could one explain the countless legends about monks encountering the devil, battling him on mountain peaks, in the middle of deserts?

Why were people worried about the devil, who was never seen in crowded cities where no one could walk without stepping on another's foot?

Andronikos thinks it's not time to pursue such questions. First he needs to survey the area, inspect, get to know his surroundings. . . .

Somehow, it occurs to him that what the mathematicians call zero is utterly — and unexpectedly — different from all the terms he has invoked until now when thinking of nothingness. God alone was able to transform chaos into order. But human beings have had to overcome zero, by one, by two, by three. . . . The forest surrounding him now is zero. His task is to arrive at one, two, three, departing from this zero. . . . To arrange one thing after another, to decipher something as far as his strength, his mind, his humanity might allow. . . .

Not long ago, he was able to resist thinking in terms of imperatives; he's determined to resist it still. He raises himself from the ground, looks up, notices that the trees become sparser on the hill. Where he stands now, they seem densely clustered, they protect one another. Perhaps he's wrong. Still, more light seems to penetrate the trees in the distance. . . . He'll see when he reaches the top of the hill.

He climbs. The sun has risen; its rays reach him through openings in the trees. Walking eastward, he estimates that noon is three hours or so away. It's neither early nor late. But if he wants to eat or perhaps rest awhile, he has to climb, descend to the shore, then climb again. There is no other way.

He tears off a piece of the bread he's been carrying in his pocket, puts it into his mouth, but only to chew it. He would run out of breath if he ate while climbing. He must pace himself, climb neither too slowly nor too quickly. He has to match the rhythm of the climb with the rhythm of his heart, his temples, his pulse. The singular, unending rhythm that God placed inside human beings. Changing but unending rhythm. Ending would mean only one thing, not two.

Death is useless, empty. Andronikos forgets the morsel in his mouth. Death must be avoided at all cost, unless the inner rhythm falters, unless God decides to stop what He put in motion, in which case nothing can be done. But if a mortal hand lunges at your body to choke that rhythm, then you can only do one thing. Grab that hand, bend that wrist with all the strength you can muster, if necessary, cut it off. No hand should have a right to another's life. Or, Andronikos reconsiders, you can do one other thing. Escape. As he's doing now. Because he doesn't have enough strength to bend that wrist, because he doesn't have enough faith to help him find the strength. . . . Escape. . . .

Once again conscious of the morsel in his mouth, Andronikos bites into the spongy lump swollen with saliva, feeling its unsavory warmth against his palate. The tree trunks are beautiful. Solid, dark, fragrant. They no longer remind him of candles melting in the heat. Neither, for that matter, of his need to find firewood. He delights in the scabrous layers upon layers of membrane-thin bark — like islets scattered among lagoons — that appear soft to the eye . . . along the deep cracks, gleaming — though slightly cloudy — trickles of pungent resin. . . .

He ought to think of the pine trees along with the

fallen pinecones — cracked, cracking, yet to crack — along with the needles that carpet the ground. The pine isn't just a tree; it's nature itself, an entire life cycle, earth beneath, sky above. Scattered among the blackened, dried-out pinecones are green ones, inexplicably fallen — incipient lives, interrupted dreams. . . . As long as it's the harsh wind or the sun rather than anything else that has caused their fall. As long as no hand has plucked them from the branches. . . .

He considers tearing off another piece of the bread, but decides to wait. It's laughable to be concerned about pinecones when wheat gets plowed, lambs are slaughtered. The pinecone, too, could be useful at times; so if you can't find one on the ground, you pluck it. Humans are sovereign, are they not? Has God not created everything to sustain human life? The senile aside, no one would dispute this most basic fact, Andronikos thinks. He wants to consider disputing it. He fails. Nevertheless, he has allowed the question to enter his mind. He closes his eyes, wants to think of something else instead. Because if one can dispute this most basic fact, then what remains? Surely, there would still be no justification for humans exploiting other humans. It's utterly indefensible.

God did not create humans for them to become each other's playthings. True, but what if it pleases us to think otherwise, with the pride the devil has instilled in us. . . . His temples throbbing, Andronikos realizes that he hasn't drunk water for hours. But his clay pitcher is still on the shore, inside the boat. . . . The water in the pitcher would last him for two days, three at the most. After that, it would become stale, infested. Andronikos had filled his pitcher at the well in the center of the village where he'd obtained the boat. It would be difficult to ration water in this heat. He should have thought sooner about finding water. The task is clearly more important than climbing the hill. Not just water, but the spring that Andronikos remembers reading about in a book by an ascetic monk. The burbling spring described by the monk ought to be somewhere around here. Andronikos will have to find it in order to remain on the island. . . .

To remain here. If he has to leave because he couldn't find water, he will end up having wasted his days wandering. He'll have to postpone settling some place, doing something. Not much will change, except for the place, although at this moment he can't think of where. Even the opposite shore seems to be fading from his view. . . . Returning to the city would be — should be — unthinkable. He doesn't want to wander around aimlessly. As for doing something. . . .

Creature of habit. The human being cannot live without thinking of doing something. Yet, to do something, say, to keep bees, to raise chickens, birds, sheep, or to grow plants, vegetables, fruits. . . . He laughs. One would need the world to do these things. Eggs, chicks, seeds, saplings. He could find these in one of the villages across the sea. But he would need money to buy them. If he tells the villagers that he's a monk, they might laugh at the kind of monk he is; if he doesn't, they would grow suspicious. In these times, the villagers would have to be more suspicious than everyone else.

This is not the time to think about them. Hill, water, shelter. Rather, water, hill, shelter. There is no other way.

A few rocks come into view through the trees. Moss covering the rocks. The books had described the moss as edible. It both curbs hunger, quenches thirst. There's still time before he has to try it.

Andronikos listens. Breeze, rustling leaves, wings beating, seagull cries, crickets beginning to chirr reluctantly. He notices heather growing among the rocks. Even if there is a stream, he wouldn't be able to hear it. He knows there is no rolling or cascading water on this island. He should keep moving his feet. Steadily, without pausing.

The rocks now seem like they're stacked one over the other, step upon step. A path, a stairway of sorts. Bordered with moss. Covered with pine needles, cones, dry, perfectly preserved shells of insects, which you couldn't find in the city, where they would be stepped on, squashed, trampled over time into dust. Not here.

The city. . . . What's happening there right now, he wonders. Who is being trampled on? What is being smashed, burned in the streets? How, by what means? His friends who didn't see him among the brothers this morning, how did they react to his absence? Did they hurry to inform the abbot? Or did they wait? If they waited, what did they wait for? If they informed, what did they say?

They must have waited until the start of the general council, which the abbot was supposed to lead immediately following the morning mass. Before the entire community, each monk was expected to come forward to renounce the old belief, affirm that his eyes had at last opened to the dreadful sin of idolatry, swear never to allow himself or others to commit such a sin. That's when his escape, rather, his absence, would be noticed. Only two monks would know that he had escaped. Ioakim. Andreas. They would have figured it out, recalling his agitated state the day before, his sudden request for dispensation to visit the city, his anxious, hesitant voice. . . . His absence at the evening mass might have led them to think that he had stayed in his cell, but the morning would have suggested otherwise. In any case, if they waited until the general council, it was probably not because they wanted him to gain time, but because they didn't know how to react. Once the news of his escape circulated, he would be called "hero" by those who liked him, "traitor" by those who didn't. Those who disliked him. . . .

The woods lead to a sudden clearing to his left. Andronikos climbs a rock squeezed between two clumps of trees. The sea. The blue, wide, calm, shimmering sea. Blue. Singular, defiant, solitary, a shade that overpowers the blue of Mother Mary's cloak as depicted in the paintings. Blue, without the red, the green or the gold. He recognizes the small, odd-shaped rocky mass across from the island. It, too, is known as an island but one that has no water. Parched, bare, except for the famished shrubs. Beyond that island, far ahead, is the hazy outline of the opposite shore immersed in mist. The village where he got the boat, his point of departure, is now a green speck in the horizon. If he didn't know it, know it by heart, he wouldn't be able to spot it from here. Slowly, very slowly, he turns his head to the left. As if he's frightened, reluctant. In the mist, at a spot somewhat darker than the others, hundreds of people gathered under the domes renouncing the old, embracing the new....

He is no hero. He is standing somewhere entirely beyond heroism.

But those who disliked him ... why did they? There had been, on occasion, a few who wanted a closer relationship with him. He never encouraged them. In the monastery everyone was a brother, which was enough; Andronikos didn't care to get any closer. For quite some time, he has avoided joining in their debates. Because the debates don't interest him. The points of disagreement are obvious from the start, therefore not even worth debating. Far from leading to any new conclusions, the debates merely provide a few people with the license to invoke certain venerated names, cloak themselves in those venerated shadows — while never failing to insinuate "in my view" into every sentence — and endlessly browbeat their listener with immeasurable, implausible nonsense. That's all they accomplish. Accomplished. He must now construct his sentences in the past tense.

Andronikos was seized with terror at first. He didn't participate in these debates, didn't want to, no longer could. Worse still, he felt no urge or desire. Because — and this is what terrified him — he didn't believe the topics themselves were important or necessary. Debating them was absurd. It seemed that people abandoned the fundamentals, talked instead about minutiae. It was like disregarding a building's foundation, arguing instead about the color or shape of its roof tiles.

He was upset with himself. If he found his brothers' priorities lacking, he should have been able to speak his mind. He did on two or three occasions. The monks turned to look at him, laughed, dismissed him with a few stern rejoinders. But later they began regarding him with suspicion.

In all likelihood, these brothers would have no misgivings about declaring steadfast loyalty to a new form of belief. They would probably call him a "traitor." "Traitor." Because he escaped. Or was he misjudging them, assigning them sins they weren't guilty of?

What about those who liked him? Ioakim? Andreas?

Andronikos stands up on the rock from which he's been gazing dreamily at the sea, the opposite shore.

Ioakim, young but mild-mannered. His blond hair with tones of brown cast by the shadows of his curls, his curly beard, his mustache, blond, red, all the shades in between. Sweet-tempered Ioakim. The shy novice who, in the early days, kept his distance from the monks, who learned little by little to slant the corner of his lips as if to smile, who learned to smile, to delve into his being, to ask himself questions, to accept answers after weighing them. Ioakim. Now in the grand assembly, it may be his turn. It wouldn't take much — it can't — for forty monks to swear an oath a few sentences long.

Or perhaps Andronikos' absence had prolonged the ceremony.

If Ioakim has already come forward, he must have done so by taking a few hesitant steps; he must have cleared his throat a few times, then sworn the oath with a steady but soft voice.

Perhaps he's angry with Andronikos.

Because he left without telling Ioakim, without taking Ioakim along, because he didn't trust him enough to tell him where he was going.

Andronikos wanted to take this journey alone. He didn't want to drag anyone into his ordeal.

This is why he first went to Galata, purchased his provisions, arranged with one of the sailors there to take him to Chalcedon. The boat carrying goods to Nikomedeia would drop him off in Chalcedon. Only one of the passengers might have recognized him. A textile merchant who had been among his childhood friends. They had played on the street, swum together. . . . One of them.

Andronikos had recognized him. He was now a middle-aged man with a conspicuous girth; laughing heartily, he kept adjusting his bright-colored garments, as if to draw attention to his success as a businessman. Andronikos made sure to keep a safe distance. The man would probably not have recognized — not that it would have mattered if he did — this fugitive monk with the long beard, his hood drawn over his long brown hair, graying in places, his discolored robe now more deep-green, deep-purple than black, like the variegated backs of crows.

But Ioakim would not have been able to figure out Andronikos' whereabouts, no matter how hard he tried.

It's almost high noon. Andronikos has to climb down from the rock to resume his walk.

What he's doing is madness. The shimmering surface of the sea begins to tire his gaze. Time passes. It must be easier to walk along the rocks.

The rocks rise like steps. The crickets have become rowdier, sending out a dizzying drone. The scent of the breeze grows intense. The brush gives off a heavy, sharp, honey-scented odor. The pine, infused with heat, mixes the two scents into one, spreads it on the air.

O God, will I manage to find the spring soon? asks Andronikos.... He hears his voice echoing back. He hasn't noticed that he spoke out loud. He should pay attention to this. One should always know whether he is speaking out loud or thinking to himself.

The sunlight flowing through the openings among the trees is scalding. Andronikos remains quiet. Making sure to keep his thoughts to himself, he continues to climb the hill. Ioakim can't find him. Ioakim must be angry that Andronikos left without telling him. Ioakim must have taken the oath, pledging his steadfast loyalty to the new creed.

In recent days, Ioakim had been searching Andronikos' mind, trying to gauge from him the right course of action, should the rumors that had been circulating turn out to be true.

According to these rumors, the decree was firm. Praying in front of painted images, kissing them, or expecting anything from them, was nothing short of idolatry. For some time now the people in the Eastern Provinces had been denouncing such practices, which, in their view, paved the surest path to perdition. Then there were the Arabs — a source of tensions for the state, known for their hostility toward painted images. As to why the Byzantine emperor would worry himself so much with these matters, it was not exactly clear. The decree deemed it unthinkable for a religion that forbade the worship of idols to make idolatry a part of worship in its churches. About the same time, statements had begun circulating to the effect that the Church had never openly or formally espoused a favorable position toward painted images. If this was the position of the Church, then why were the churches flooded with icons? Why did everyone, from the Emperor all the way down to the beggar on the street, believe that these icons were sacred? Ioakim was trying to understand this. Andronikos would have preferred not to even think about it, although he, too, was at a loss.

Idols, icons, all forms of painted images would be removed, a form of worship free of idolatry would be revived. This was the basis of true religion. The icons would not just be removed. When previously attempted, this measure had had bloody consequences, worse still, right at the palace gates. True, that episode wasn't only about painted images, there was also a widespread sentiment among the terrified public that the Emperor was almost attempting to put himself in the place of Jesus. The Emperor, it was said, could ill afford to encourage such unrest again. The icons would be burned.

Burned. In order to squelch dissent, to discipline the resistant subjects, to discourage blind devotion to the old creed, now or in the future.

There were other rumors. Other decrees were imminent. The unusual specificity of some of the rumors suggested that there were disagreements — at least in the beginning — among those making the decisions.

According to the same rumors, the Emperor had convened the Supreme Council, seeking its approval of the decree. When the Bishop had objected, he was summarily dismissed. The Emperor had appointed an acquiescent priest to serve as the new Bishop. The rumors were spreading throughout the capital, even though palace officials had taken great care to augment the news about the Bishop's dismissal with statements about his ill health.

Who knows, perhaps the Council was unanimous only in appearance. Perhaps the reality was different. The rumors hinted at ulterior motives behind the decree. A recent visit to Byzantium by leaders of the Eastern Provinces was invoked as proof of their role in the decree. They had come to inform the Emperor of the renewed campaign in the East against icons, idolatry. The Emperor had to trust the Eastern armies against the Arabs. The Eastern armies were categorically against idolatry.

These were the rumors, tangled threads of truth, speculation, wandering the streets of the capital.

For Andronikos, these explanations, secret or public, carried no significance. . . . He was concerned instead with what he would do, what he had to do, on the day the decree went into effect.

Suddenly, the wind whips Andronikos' face. He stops, feels the dampness of his skin in the cool air, noting that he's been sweating. But that's also when he feels once more the pain in the soles of his feet. He had forgotten his soles scarred by the sharp rocks of the shore. If he can find water, he'll soak his soles to ease the pain. Until then, he has to endure.

He must walk, since he can do nothing else. But first he unties his shoelaces. Removing his shoes, he shakes out the pine needles, the tiny stones collected in them. He puts on his shoes, reties the laces.

Andreas. After speaking his mind during countless debates, Andreas had fallen silent only recently, maybe in the last few years. But lately, his sentiments had managed to break through this silence. "At this rate, we'll go back to the age of idolatry," he had said. Because of the incident at the palace gates. On the same night when the monks heard the news about riots by the masses, specifically women, protesting the destruction of the painting of Jesus above the palace gates, the killing of the imperial officer supervising the destruction. The Emperor, in retaliation, would replace Jesus' likeness with the cross. But Andreas didn't know this. He must have expressed his opinion because he trusted Andronikos. At the time, Andreas agreed with the Emperor's decree. Yet nothing had changed at the monastery. . . .

Andreas was right in trusting Andronikos.

Andronikos was not the type of person who would take it upon himself to inform the abbot about an opinion that sharply contradicted the monastery's long-held creed. Even so, Andreas was wrong in thinking that Andronikos would agree with him. That is, if Andreas had thought about any of this.

Startled at first by Andreas' words, Andronikos had eventually managed to ask him how he'd arrived at such opinions, after all the years Andreas had worshipped in front of painted images, based his faith on those images, or at least had kept up the appearance of doing so. After a great deal of reflection, Andreas had answered. Andronikos was not entirely convinced. A person could indeed change his mind after deep, sustained reflection, but at least some evidence, even a slight hint, of this change would have shown in his face. Wasn't Andreas old enough to have formulated his opinions years ago? Or if the change had instead come unexpectedly, without any forethought, then wouldn't the dread of every imaginable consequence have led him to behave differently? That evening during mass, Andronikos hadn't noticed even the slightest change in Andreas' demeanor. Which meant that either Andreas did not disapprove of icon worship or he had lied that morning. Could it be possible that he had tried to test Andronikos? But he would have had no reason to do so. Andreas always weighed his thoughts, spoke sparingly, always told the truth. He wasn't easily excitable during conversations; one always knew that his every word was born of deep conviction.

Andronikos stops. The breeze has died down. In the

heat, the scent of holly is more dizzying than ever. Apart from the languid buzz of insects, the island is silent. In the distance, far in the distance, a faint murmur: like the dying echo of faraway waves breaking against the rocks. But the sea is calm, an unbroken surface — like liquid silver — shimmering in sunlight. This distant-sounding murmur might be from a brook nearby. Andronikos realizes that he hasn't thought of water for quite some time. The spring the monk described could be somewhere on this hill. Finding it so quickly would be much too easy. Or is he mistaken? The monk had described bathing himself, drinking water while facing the rising sun. Andronikos had forgotten this detail, even though, somehow, he's been traveling eastward since morning.

Andreas had come by the next day, resumed the conversation where they had left off. He had mentioned that the genesis of icon worship coincides with the time of the Persian wars. Andronikos didn't know whether this was true or not. For as long as he could tell, the icons had been considered sacred. Andreas had said that the Armenians value the cross more than the icons. Andronikos was surprised. Using the Armenians as an example would have occurred only to Andreas. I'm not against icons, Andreas had added, but it frightens me to think that people could invest icons with so much sacred value, that they're capable of murder for the sake of their icons. . . .

Andronikos suddenly connects these words to the content of the Emperor's decree. The decree didn't prohibit all painted images, only sacred ones. He's angry with himself. How could he not have thought of this distinction before? Why had he not broached the subject with Andreas?

Looking back, he notices that he's walked a good distance, climbed quite high above the sea level. Down below, he can only see a part of the gravel shore. Straining to see through the trees, he can't tell whether or not he's near the top of the hill. He's surrounded by trees on all sides, though the woods are less dense here than below. He probably has quite a climb ahead of him before he reaches the top. . . .

If the spring is somewhere around here, he has to find it before anything else. If it's to be found anywhere, the water that one bathes in while facing the sunrise is probably on the opposite side of the hill. But Andronikos hasn't even reached the top of the hill. So then, should he say, first the hill, then the spring?

Andronikos feels tired all of a sudden. He squats by a tree. Looking to his right, he notices a small clearing on top of a mound rising like the back of a torso. If he climbs there, he may be able to survey his surroundings better. He gets up, resumes walking. Once there, the clearing proves deceptive, though he can certainly see better what's ahead of him — the path he must take in order to reach the top of the hill. He leans against the gnarled trunk of an ancient pine tree, takes his loaf of bread from his pocket. Biting off a morsel, he begins to chew it slowly.

When rumors overtook the capital, spreading like ivy, Andronikos had thought he understood Andreas' view better. Since Andreas never strayed from the truth in his heart, he knew that worshipping icons would be perceived as idolatry, which he clearly disapproved of. That much was certain. But why he continued praying in front of the icons, Andronikos could not explain. Did Andreas favor his views, his very own views, or those of the Emperor? Which did he respect more — the Emperor's decrees or his own convictions?

Underneath all of this, there might have been ulterior calculations, certain secret intentions. . . .

Whether there had been or not, it no longer mattered

to Andronikos. It couldn't. That Andreas had continued to pray in front of the icons was probably nothing other than habitual behavior carried out while waiting for the official creed to change. This is how Andronikos understands it now. An obligatory act performed according to forms, devoid of heart or conviction. Something quite inconceivable to Andronikos. But he has no other way to understand or explain Andreas' behavior.

Andronikos puts the last morsel in his mouth. He chews slowly, deliberately, to dissolve the morsel entirely so that he won't need water to wash it down. At this point there is nothing for him to do. Except find the spring.

Had Andreas responded to the recent wave of rumors self-righteously, he would have upset Andronikos. Rather, he had said, "You know my views. What are you going to do?" Andronikos hadn't replied. He didn't know what he was supposed to do. Even the mere fact of his uncertainty should have made him realize the myriad things he should have already understood. Even on that day.

Andronikos had made the mistake of perceiving the state of unknowing or the inability to know as an article of faith. He had fooled himself into thinking so.

A while later, Ioakim had come to Andronikos, excitedly describing what he had heard. Much to his surprise, Andronikos had shown no emotion. "What are you going to do?" Ioakim had asked. Andronikos had again replied, "I don't know." He didn't know. He wanted to shout at the top of his lungs that he didn't know. That's what the very core of his being wanted to announce to the world. Later in the evening, when he'd calmed down, he had approached Ioakim; "I'm thinking," he had told him, then quickly left. Ioakim must have thought that Andronikos was caught in an inner turmoil, struggling with the gravest, the most vital questions of faith, of conscience.

Andronikos had been thinking — had begun

thinking — although about entirely different matters. That evening, the monks who'd spent the day in the capital had returned to the monastery with the latest rumors. In the neighborhoods around the palace, around the cathedral, people appeared somewhat reserved, unsure. In a neighborhood or two, some people defended the new thinking, perceiving a timely edict beneficial for all the citizens. But the monks who had traveled to the outlying areas had different observations. In those neighborhoods along the city walls, on the roads along the pastures, along the cemeteries, in the houses clustered around small chapels, the people grumbled. Just as there were some who equated the rumored events — if confirmed — with the gravest imaginable blasphemies. . . .

Time to get up. It's almost high noon. Facing east, Andronikos begins to walk toward the top of the hill. The path ahead isn't level, but it's considerably easier to walk.

. . . there were also others who sensed a conspiracy, a hidden scheme beneath the edict, arguing that the edict would most certainly serve as an excuse for some other action. Otherwise, it defied common sense to introduce such a measure virtually overnight, without apparent provocation. God knows what was really decided at those councils. . . .

The Emperor was an Easterner. His close relationship with the Eastern armies was common knowledge. His throne depended on this relationship. He could secure the welfare of the empire, as well as protect the eastern borders against the enemies, by acceding to his generals, to the wishes of the bishops in the Eastern provinces. Or else. . . .

Only recently had Andronikos become aware of this fear of the East. An Eastern ogre had laid siege to Byzantium, sending terror into the hearts of the people, overwhelming their senses, giving rise to all kinds of wild speculations. These fears, these speculations, had visited

Andronikos' mind as well. But he hadn't paid too much attention. "What if. . . ." "What if. . . ." What was the use of hinting at suspicions that couldn't be voiced, much less proven?

There were also others who viewed the Emperor's actions as an attempt to anoint himself as the absolute ruler, in place of the most hallowed eternal being, the true Lord Jesus.

To search for the truth, for a way out of this terrifying chaos, as if caught inside a dense, impenetrable fog. . . .

But Andronikos had put aside all these concerns, finished his meal before retreating to his cell. During the supper, Ioakim hadn't removed his gaze from Andronikos who had pretended to be lost in thought, deep in contemplation, in order to prevent Ioakim from following him to his cell. Entering his cell, Andronikos had locked the door, thrown his body on the mattress.

There, lying still, now asleep now awake, he'd ushered in the morning.

"New." "Creed." His mind had wrestled with these words throughout the night. He couldn't construe a relationship between them. No one had been after him. No one had asked him to recognize the "new," the "creed," or construe a relationship between them. No one had been pressuring him. Nevertheless, Andronikos had endured a mighty struggle throughout the night, as if he had to resolve all conflicts by morning in order to decide what he was supposed to do.

The trees ahead of him stand farther apart from each other. Andronikos knows that he's nearing the top of the hill. The path continues to rise, now a little more steeply. There's also an occasional breeze, but as if blown from the mouth of an oven.

All of a sudden, Andronikos feels bloated, as if he has consumed countless bowls of food. He knows he can't go on like this. If he doesn't take a nap, drink a little water, he knows he'll become sluggish, useless. Already the day is half over. He thinks that after he descends, he'll wait for the shade to fall over these parts before he returns to the hill again. . . .

But first he must climb. . . .

Around dawn, he'd awakened with a start. The cell was slowly getting brighter. He had stared at the walls, at the window. Only later did he realize that he'd fallen asleep; if only briefly, the thoughts swarming inside his head had finally been defeated by sleep. He'd felt an odd happiness somehow. What was the point, if not utter futility, of endlessly thinking without ever arriving at a decision — never mind a decision, not even a conclusion — without even the hope of arriving at one?

His reasoning had been entirely wrong, backward. He should have first asked himself this: If the rumors come true, if I must abandon everything I've believed to this day, if I must renounce everything I've done in the name of my faith, what happens if I do so? What happens if I don't? This was the real question. He shouldn't have run away, instead he should have tried to answer it. . . .

As the trees become sparser, he can see the sky through the widening spaces among them. Below him, the sea is an ever-widening expanse. His skin is burning as the warm breeze is accompanied now by the sun's scalding heat. The chirr of crickets has become an omnipresent, enveloping vibration, noticeable only when it dies down every so often. He wonders whether or not the countless invisible insects can see him, if these intervals of silence mean that he is a fearsome intruder among them.

Andronikos pauses, then, relaxing, begins to smile. In the distance, a small ship with its billowing sail is approaching the city. It must be coming from the Nicomedeia gulf, probably carrying provisions. Perhaps wine, maybe olives or olive oil. The ship's crewmen would not be able to make him out from this far away. Besides, it makes no difference if they can. . . . But above all, Andronikos must rid himself of the feeling of being pursued. Had he stayed one more day in the city, it's certain he would have been pursued. He might have been. He might have had to run away. But since he's here now, since he's come as far as he has before anyone had the time to force him to flee, it means he has escaped. He doesn't have to worry.

The sky is clear, cloudless. Perfectly blue, without a hint of humidity. The white sail, set against the black-red streaks of the ship along the luminescent blue sea, looks like a separate living being, agile, moving to its own fancy. The opposite shore is covered in a veil of mist, though he can still discern clusters of vegetation.

Andronikos' gaze traces an imaginary line from rock to rock, extending toward the city. He pauses again. But this time he isn't visited by the sensation or the fear of being pursued.

Among the domes, black clouds of smoke rise through the mist. He stares at the billows of smoke. Fires start easily in this season, especially at this hour. Because the smoke can be seen from such a distance, the fires must have spread quickly today. But so many of them at once. . . .

Andronikos stops, even hesitates to think. Perhaps the fear he's been trying to ward off isn't groundless after all. He may be outside the reach of this fear, but in the city. . . .

Perhaps they're burning the icons, the monasteries of the resistant monks who refuse to embrace the new creed, perhaps the houses in the acrimonious neighborhoods that had defied the edict in the early days. In the name of true faith.

None of this should matter to him anymore. Neither

the places set on fire nor the people setting the fires — both sides playing their respective parts in the name of their faith. Since. . . .

Turning away from the view, he begins to walk, without thinking of his fatigue, the heat, water or sleep, feeling something akin to rage. This, too, is among the emotions, the habits, that he must purge from his heart. He should walk fast. He can see the top of the hill. He can't drag his exhausted body any farther. But he must reach the top.

Once there, he finds himself staring at a narrow clearing, except for the occasional solitary tree murmuring, creaking with the breeze. The ground is no longer covered with pine needles. There are wide, smooth rocks around him, stretches of exposed earth. The sun, unhindered, uninhibited, scorches the terrain.

The spring must be somewhere near, Andronikos thinks. He should look for it around here. He has arrived at the highest point, the island's peak.

Below him is an ever-deepening sea of pine, vibrant, sonorous, as if it were the dwelling place of all the island's chirring insects, all the songbirds. Straight ahead is the island's second, much smaller hill, its top densely packed with pine trees. Dark green. On two sides, the sea — wide, flat, shimmering as if melting. . . . The seagulls fly behind the little ship on its way to the city. From time to time he can hear their sorrowful shrieks that recall the cries of a child pulled too soon from his mother's breast.

Now, farther away, the seagulls circle the sky. What other bird would fly in the sweltering midday heat?

Andronikos surveys the opposite side of the hill where the trees begin much further down, at the bottom of a natural stairway of rocks descending step after step. Eastward. Along the southern slope there are even larger rocks, but clustered more closely together, allowing the trees to begin at a higher elevation. Andronikos decides to take the eastern slope, where, if he remembers correctly what he once read, he's more likely to find the spring. . . .

Andronikos had experienced a sense of peace once he'd figured out which question he should answer first. The following day, he had tried not to think altogether, to live instead his everyday life, perform his everyday deeds. Ioakim had kept an anxious watch all day, trying to catch his glance, yet, all the same, obviously hesitant to approach him with any questions. As for Andreas, he had gone about his everyday routine, befitting a man who knew exactly the grounds for his every action.

By evening the speculation had gotten all the more out of control, giving way to a widespread sentiment that the decree had been authorized, that it would be announced soon, followed by the measures to enforce it, along with those aimed at squelching dissent.

After vespers, Andronikos had surrendered to his thoughts again, his question gnawing at his conscience. But by dawn, one point had become glaringly obvious: If he embraced the new creed, his action would allow him once again to conform, to obey, to affirm the bond that united him with his fellow human beings, although this particular action would also contradict all his previous actions that had been guided by faith, by inner conviction. It would force him to abandon all his customs, to repudiate the very faith heretofore expressed through these customs. He was attached to the past, he had realized; it would not be easy to abandon the old faith.

That next day, too, he had continued performing his usual tasks as before. But one thing about his behavior had changed: He'd begun to think of his actions in light of the new decree. Looking at the icons, he'd tried to see them stripped of their sacred nature. Crossing himself in front of them, he'd tried to imagine a being who existed beyond the icons, who was separate, who was released from the figures in them.

He had tried to imagine the same thing happening throughout the churches, then throughout the city that contained hundreds of chapels, churches, cathedrals, then throughout the territories surrounding the capital, throughout the entire state of Byzantium, the entire realm of the Emperor.

Countless icons had appeared before his eyes. Icon upon icon, a massive pile growing into an immense mountain, a gilded conflagration, an ocean of gold spreading out with every passing hour that marked on earth the sun's trajectory across the heavens. Churches had appeared before his eyes. One at first, then a few, then tens, hundreds of churches. Their walls stripped bare, the cloudy whiteness of the spaces where the icons had hung for years. He had thought of the great cathedral built in the name of Holy Wisdom, its ceilings, domes, arches, walls replete with icons, mosaics, inch after inch of dazzling tiles set in plaster, depicting hallowed figures, the largest Cathedral in the state, the largest in the world. . . . Those images could not be taken down. At the most, they would be whitewashed or plastered over.

But only one thing could vanquish that massive, mountain-like, ocean-like heap.

Fire.

Andronikos had thought of fire that evening. When the sun was setting.

All day he had tried to imagine the change, its magnitude. It was a difficult task. Exhausting. What about the sponsors of the decree? Had they thought this way, or as much? By the time night arrived, Andronikos had concluded that they hadn't, couldn't have.

They belonged to the race of men who ordered fire without flinching, if fire simply satisfied their will. How the fire would be set, how the icons would be collected, burned to ashes, those matters were up to their underlings to decide. The subordinates, possibly even those under them, those lackeys would have to figure out the details. Not the rulers. But Andronikos was terrified for having thought of fire himself. In the morning, he had woken up panic-stricken, afraid of himself, for being capable of thinking of fire.

He pulls himself together.

Andronikos isn't sure how long he's been sitting on this rock. He shouldn't let his mind wander off. He's feeling dizzy. He has to find the spring. Here, somewhere among the rocks facing east. If he can't find it. But he must.

He descends a little further, his eyes, ever more attentive, fixed on the ground. Soon, he makes it past the rocks, stops near the edge of the woods. He looks back. His head is aching, so is his neck. He's drenched in sweat. His vision is blurred from having stared too long at the sea. He can't make out the shapes around him. The intense heat makes the air shimmer, further blurring the outlines of the rocks, the bushes around him.

The next step was obvious: Since he could not reconcile himself to the changes or the injunctions, then he had to reject them. But what would happen then?

At the end of one more night, all of Andronikos' questions had been answered; he had greeted the morning with an unmistakable sense of clarity.

What agony he had had to endure to get there. The harrowing headaches, the burning eyes — as today — that had been his unrelenting tormentors. Nothing could have been worse, not even being yoked to a mill for three days, without bread or water, surviving on nothing but the grating millstones, the creaking wooden shafts.

In the end, the path had opened.

The path of departure. The path of escape.

He wouldn't abandon his faith in order to endure the new. In two days, when the edict took effect, Andronikos could well imagine the fate that awaited him. At the least, he would be sent to the dungeon, to bring him back to his senses. Before too long, he might even be excommunicated, or worse still, executed.

He knew well that nothing was ever spared those who defied the Emperor, his commands, or his laws on matters of religious faith, in order to insure that traitors felt infinite remorse before facing their death. Even children playing on the street knew of the varieties of torture carried out in the Emperor's dungeons. Had he not played those torture games as a child, in remote alleys, in vacant fields, at the edges of cemeteries? The children of Byzantium enjoyed playing war or playing bandits as often as they did playing those torture games.

Yet, concerning his fate, Andronikos had thought only as far as the dungeons without taking into account the possibility of excommunication, torture or execution. He was sure that he would be sent to the dungeon, probably within days of his arrest. This was a fact, straightforward, certain.

If I am so afraid of the dungeon, he had said to himself while weighing his options, if I consider the dungeon such a terrifying prospect, how can I claim, how can I even think, that my faith is strong? That it is this strength that compels me to refuse to abandon my faith? For years, I've experienced faith as a monk, as a man of religion, I've perceived my devotion as something beyond all doubt. I reproached people, challenged them, for not believing enough. I tried to compel, convince the rich as well as the poor that faith is above all the wealth, all the suffering of this world. Have I done this out of habit, because I've been used to thinking or speaking in no other manner? because I've carried out my duties with no more reflection or afterthought than drinking, eating, walking or sleeping?

As a man of the faith, as its messenger, a human model of piety among humans, I've rebuked some, praised others, measured their faith, weighed the merit of their deeds, judged the extent of their devotion or transgressions, while I've never thought of searching into myself. I must have considered myself infallible. In other words, for years, I must have spoken of love without ever distinguishing love from reverence, reverence from the habit of kissing hands; I must have expected others to kiss my hand just as they kiss the icons, or the cross. In the homes I've visited, among the people I've met, I've favored certain forms of love while censuring others; there have been occasions when I've withheld the blessing asked of me. All along, I've never questioned my actions. All along, I've performed the rites in the name of the faith that I was raised in, the faith that shaped my being, the faith that, one day, appointed me its messenger.

Now what is being eliminated, destroyed, is not the faith itself but a significant part of its observance. If the faith remains unharmed but its observance, mirrored in every moment of my life, changes; if I accept this change as if changing shirts, I will have lied for years. My life will have been one unbroken lie.

Andronikos feels a strange duality. He is thinking these thoughts, remembering them, while at the same time he is observing himself thinking, remembering. As though watching someone else from a distance. Confused, he can't decide whether these thoughts belong to that fateful night when he made up his mind to escape, or to last night when he crossed the sea, or if he's just thought them now. He remembers the uneasy feeling from mornings past when he would wake up conscious of the details of a dream he couldn't place in time, whether it was a dream he'd had the night before, or a week or years ago. Andronikos tries to shake off his confusion, struggles to escape the disquieting maze of his thoughts. He feels tired, sleepy. That night. . . .

No, that night, fear had superseded everything, that night I was thinking of, above all else, the dungeon. It wasn't until the night I spent in the boat, rowing, fighting off sleep, that I thought, hour after long hour, about my rights, about the rights of others. This recognition animates Andronikos, he can resist sleep a little longer.

I will have lied for years, my life will have been one unbroken lie. I know I don't want to allow this to happen. But since the idea of being thrown in the dungeon terrifies me, I must also realize how weak, how fragile are the ties that connect me to this faith that I presumably value.

Of course, this realization had not been easy, yet there was another stage of understanding that required coming to grips with his realization, feeling its weight in his brain, in his hands, his arms, his veins. Ah, how tenuous his faith had been! That's when Andronikos had closed his eyes, begging the Lord to take his life, to cast his useless body into the deepest recesses of the earth. But the earth hadn't opened to swallow him. He had not died. God had not accepted his plea. That's when he had opened his eyes, telling himself, I must live out my fate, I must experience this suffering, drink it to its last drop. It was fine to give this advice to others. Now I must listen, endure, drink my shame to its last drop.

Then I must have been lying all these years — even if unintentionally, unknowingly.

The thought had made his head spin. It's still spinning now. But now he's also suffering from sleeplessness, hunger, knowing at the same time that the thought will forever keep his head spinning, forever anxious.

Should I invent a new lie, or should I, in the glaring light of the old lie, obliterate all chances of lying?

This question had preoccupied him for a long time.

If I'm afraid of the dungeon, it means that I must not be able to feel the weight of my faith, that I'm unwilling to bear its burden on my shoulders.

Icy, numbing thoughts. As on that night in his cell, after he had experienced the first spell of cold sweat. He's in that liminal space when a person no longer feels the weight of his body — as if it has vanished and he is about to enter a state of being made of nothing but pure thought. . . . Yet, this, too, is a lie. The icy numbness is there, but Andronikos is so aware of the weight of his body that he can't be aware of anything else, he can't tell whether or not there is anything more than this willful corporeality. Even if there is, he knows that he is not, that he cannot be, aware, that he will never be aware.

Can a person be considered faithful if he can't even bear the thought of being thrown in the dungeon because of his faith? It means that, in reality, I am not faithful. It means that I have lied for years — unconsciously, unknowingly. I have lived my lie, forced others to live it with me. I didn't just deceive myself, I also deceived everyone else.

Andronikos is still confused, can't say whether these thoughts belong to that night in his cell, or last night, or to the present. He does recall distinctly the eerie feeling of urgency, the fear of running late that accompanied these thoughts. He remembers sensing the presence of something, no, someone, urging him, as if telling him to hurry, to move faster, faster still. True, he couldn't escape the thoughts, but did he not have the power to hurry them through his mind, to feel less shame, though doing so would have been yet another source of shame? Thoughts begetting thoughts, do they ever end?

If I realize only now that what I perceived as my faith was nothing more than a habit of the mind, if I could not find the inner strength to face the dungeon without fear, how can I believe in something new? Deceive myself once again, along with everyone else?

His mind is quite lucid now. Was it so on that night? He grins with self-contempt. He has every right to feel this way, he can at least admit to this feeling. . . .

There was only one way out for Andronikos, to leave, to escape. To find a place where he won't, where he won't have to, deceive himself or others. A place that will ask nothing of him — neither to accept a new faith nor even to live according to his old faith. A place that accommodates nothing of what Andronikos has come to symbolize in his community.

He is aware that all of these are afterthoughts, add-ons, explanations after the fact, sundry comments, rationalizations to justify himself in his own eyes. Living life like writing a book. He is aware of it. All too well.

Andronikos had entered the monastery much too young to have experienced any other life; raised from seed as a monk, he could not imagine finding another occupation, a different livelihood, marrying or fathering children. The idea of renouncing his vow of celibacy seems to him, even now, repugnant, perfidious.

He doesn't want others to think that he has left to escape celibacy. He wants nothing to do with even the idea of marriage. He has not known the female body since the day he took his vows. That day, too, is now in the distant past, even the memory of which is difficult to retrieve. . . .

Andronikos forces himself to open his eyes. His vision is hazy at first, as if he's staring into a fog, but gradually everything comes into focus, becomes clear. Among the clean, distinct shapes, if he could just see a tuft of fresh green, apart from the holly, apart from the dusty bushes, just a handful of green brighter than the evergreen. . . .

He sees it. At the bottom of the steep rocks, where the incline begins to bend southward. He walks there, with his splitting headache, his burning eyes, his aching soles, his scarred, stinging knees, he walks. The spring is there.

He sees it. A quiet little stream. . . .

He should dig around its mouth, find a couple of flat stones to build a trough; he should bathe at sunrise, fill his pitcher. Then he should try to grow a little garden for himself. . . .

He comes back to himself.

Splashing his face with cold water had calmed him somewhat. His eyes were still burning, his head still pounding, but because he knew what he had to do next, he was able to find the inner strength to figure out how.

He had to escape. Run away, far away, anticipating the day when he would find the means necessary to start life anew. . . .

It wasn't until dawn that Andronikos had seized upon the idea of escaping to the island that even the hermit monks no longer inhabited; the palace people, contemptuous of everything that belonged to the past, had long dismissed the island as a place unfit for afternoon excursions, let alone for extended sojourns.

He lifts his head, feels the water running through his hair, face, beard, down to his neck, shoulders, chest. He can't imagine a greater pleasure than what he is experiencing right now.

He can hear his voice again. He wants to hear his voice. He speaks, certain that he'll hear himself. His eyes are still burning but the pounding inside his head seems to have abated, dissolved in the water. Leaning forward, he splashes his face, cups his hands, pours water down his shoulders. Straightening up, he lets the water flow between his shoulder blades, along his spine, down to his tailbone.

Above him, the sun watches aimlessly. The breeze is warm. The water flows endlessly. Over his body. Inside him. In the hollow of his mortal frame. Reverberations.

It would be good to eat something but his provisions are in his sack, which he has left at the foot of the hill. He has water; he's made it to the top of the hill. Perhaps he should think about building a shelter.

The ground is covered with nothing but gravel. Further down the southern slope, he sees tall rocks, some in clusters, others loose, standing alone. If he can find two rocks standing close to one another, it won't be too difficult to build a third wall. That's what Andronikos is looking for.

Soon enough he spots two large rocks positioned even better than he had hoped, set so closely together that they almost form a niche shaped like a large arrowhead. The wider opening faces south, while the narrow gap set against the slope is naturally protected by the hill. For now, he can use tree branches to build a roof, which wouldn't keep the rain out, but a sturdier roof would require strenuous work — a task best left for another day. If he combs his surroundings, he'll certainly find enough stones to build the third wall.

It occurs to him that he'll need mortar to set the stones. He hadn't thought about this before. Never mind the mortar, he hadn't thought about what he would do once he reached the island.

All he knew at the time was that he would have to go down to the harbor, take a boat to Galata, where he would try to secure everything he needed for his journey. A monk making unusual purchases in the center of the capital could have been — at the very least — a source of ugly mockery.

Andronikos had thought so at the time, but now he knows that it was not the prospect of mockery but an ugly, hideous fear that had spurred him. He is aware of it now, though oddly he's not ashamed anymore. I shouldn't be ashamed of my fear, he tells himself. Above all else, wasn't it fear that motivated me? My fear is on my side, it's part of my being, perhaps the most vital part. Out of fear, what have I tried to defend? Which part of my life is worth defending? The questions strike him as irrelevant. Andronikos doesn't think that any part of him is worth defending. Fear of torture is what he knows, nothing more. He has no choice but to recognize this fear as his own; if he can't be proud of it, at least he ought to not feel ashamed of it.

Once he made his purchases in Galata, it wouldn't be difficult to find a boatman willing to take him to Chalcedon. Once he got there, a peasant would certainly be agreeable to offering him a horse, or at least, selling him one. Andronikos would need money. To find it. . . .

He wouldn't have to lie. The oil merchant Nicholas would give him the money without asking for an explanation. He was an old friend who had helped him once or twice in the past. Besides, in the current climate, Nicholas wouldn't hesitate to give him the money, what little Andronikos needed. Perhaps Nicholas would even understand what Andronikos was about to do; but he would not betray his friend.

The trust that Andronikos felt in Nicholas fills him with joy. He is the friend I love the most. I wasn't even aware of it. So much I wasn't aware of. . . .

He'd ended up spending very little of the money he had asked from Nicholas. The remainder was still in his sack, tucked under his provisions. The peasant in Chalcedon had told him that he would be satisfied with the honor of having helped a man of God, if Andronikos agreed to take the horse to his cousin in Pendik. The peasant's cousin who had received the horse had offered Andronikos the use of his boat. It wasn't a big boat, the cousin had told him, he no longer used it for fishing since his brother-in-law's boat served them better. Still, it would have been a sin to let the old boat rot away. Buyers were hard to come by these days. The venerable monk could keep the boat for as long as he needed; if one day he decided to, he knew where to bring it back. . . .

At the end of the speech, Andronikos had blessed the garrulous man, thanked him, then left. Then, an hour into his journey, Andronikos had thought that blessing the poor man had been a mistake. An error in judgment, a deception. Here he was escaping from the oppressive weight of a faith that he could no longer embrace, while he was also practicing one of its sacraments, in turn deceiving someone else.

His clothes, his deception began with his clothes — the only ones he's worn all his adult life. His robe, already old, faded, would get older still on the island. One of these days, he will have to find different clothes for himself, but trying to decide what he might choose to wear is an exercise in futility.

The sun continues to move along its daily arc across the sky, it doesn't wait for Andronikos. He ought to start descending the hill, first climb back up, then down along the other side. . . .

Andronikos doesn't dismiss the significance of the decision about the clothing he'll eventually choose for himself. The task will require self-reflection, an understanding of his identity stripped of the monk's attire. At the same time, he reproaches himself for postponing the decision until his robe is in tatters, until, finally pinned down, he can't postpone the decision any longer, in short, for his unrelenting procrastination.

For now, there are more important concerns: such as shelter, such as the setting sun, his hunger, the need to resist despair, remorse, the sense of defeat lying in wait for him behind the rocks, the need to prevail, to move forward. . . .

If he is to live on this island — not as if inhabiting a dream but the way he has lived for years at the monastery — if his life is to have some semblance of authenticity, he'll have to establish certain modest habits. Such as eating his meals at certain times, drinking water, sleeping, waking up, preparing his food, praying, working the soil. . . . Praying should continue to be among these modest habits. He should pray perhaps not like a monk but like an ordinary person, like one of the thousands, tens of thousands, hundreds of thousands of people living throughout the realms of the empire.

He should certainly work the soil. Even though he doesn't yet know how, or which tools to make, he should work the soil. Not just to grow things he can eat but to foster those habits intended to make living easier. This way, he will have discrete tasks to complete, each task separated from the other by the unoccupied hours in between. . . . To fill those hours, he'll have to find other tasks, perhaps give himself to introspection, weigh, sift the whims of his mind, perhaps write something, or grow flowers.

He laughs.

Grow flowers. . . . Isn't it laughable for a man — a man of God, no less — who is running away from religious persecution to put everything aside so he can indulge in growing flowers? Still, it would be far better than most occupations he had often observed among hundreds of people in the capital — such as drinking oneself to the point of stupor, fighting on the street or in the family, beating people or getting beaten, robbery, picking pockets, prostituting women, or committing arson on orders of one's superiors. Far better than any of these. . . .

It must be late in the day. Andronikos isn't aware that

he has been walking. He finds himself among the pine trees. The breeze is somewhat cooler this time, ushering in less the pine scent or that of the spice bushes than the smell of the sea. He stops. The breeze feels good, like a soft hand caressing his face, his neck. Like soft hands covered with translucent hairs, blond or dark down. He mustn't allow such notions to visit his mind; he must drive them out as soon as they make themselves known.

There among the pine trees, a crow stands a few steps away from him. A young, coal-black crow with coppery streaks across its showy plumage, casting a sideways glance at Andronikos. It hops a step or two; Andronikos takes a single step toward the bird, then, stopping, he lowers his body to the ground slowly, almost imperceptibly, so as not to scare the bird away. He's not interested in catching it — even if he can — and eating it. The crow moves slightly toward him but, suddenly taking wing, perches on a low branch. Perhaps it's a lost crow, Andronikos thinks. Then he hears the seagulls' piercing cry coming from a remote part of the island. The lucky scavengers' cry. The crow takes flight again, this time toward the sound of the seagulls, as if sharing in their satisfaction.

Rising to his feet, Andronikos resumes his descent. If only he had some wine. . . . He laughs, knowing that he's talking nonsense.

He thinks that he is not a man of adventure. In order to chase after adventure, one must have a strong heart, courage, he must be able to unchain himself from habits; rather, he must avoid developing habits. Andronikos is not such a man.

His courage, his heart, shows itself only when he's cornered. When he is truly cornered, when acting decisively is absolutely his last recourse, only then does he muster the will, albeit a little foolhardy, to step forward. Later, he neither regrets his action nor dreads its consequences;

rather, he's amazed that he was able to act at all. Can this even be called courage. . . . So entirely different from the courage of the adventurous spirits.

The man who loves adventure can live alone; he was created to live alone. As a child, Andronikos had heard plenty of stories about seafarers or fishermen . . . Now he truly understands these men. Solitude appeals to him, too. He always preferred being with people only when he wanted to, avoiding their company when he didn't. But what he truly loves, what he desires the most, is to be able to isolate himself while surrounded by people, to stand alone among them because he wants to. He is keenly aware of this desire. Solitude becomes all the more enjoyable when it isn't compulsory. But Andronikos also feels something else, something difficult to describe . . . It's as if his peace of mind depends on the presence of others making itself felt, even if from a distance. He needs other people, even if only to distance himself from them. Yes, something like this, more or less. His type of solitude needs the presence of others. Now that he is truly alone, far away from the capital, he's seeking to recover his life in the city, the ordinary habits of city life; the realization frightens him. Andronikos tries to suppress the disquieting thoughts by reminding himself of his more basic needs at the moment — shelter, food, water.

He wants to finish building his shelter, create tasks for himself, create around them an orderly existence so that, concerned less with the small details of everyday life, he can find time instead for other things. For years, these other things used to include praying, blessing, contemplating theology or the wisdom of the ancients, comforting the afflicted whom no one else cared to or had time to comfort.

Now he can grow flowers or do something else, anything. . . .

Even if faith is removed from his life's equation.

He looks back. The hilltop is far away now. Ahead of him, the shadows of the pine trees stretch out like an immense fan. Through an opening among the three branches, he spies a seagull, large, white, graceful, gliding peacefully. The sea is barely visible from where he stands. Andronikos had not realized until now that he has been walking along a trail — if not a path — a faint depression, maybe formed by an old stream.... Or maybe by fishermen who occasionally visit the island, walk all the way up here. But he should follow the trail, find out where it leads, where it ends.

The seagulls must have finished foraging by now. The crow also must have satisfied its hunger with their leftovers. If so, Andronikos thinks, the bird would fly back here, find him again.

The island is perfectly still. Not a trace of mist impedes the view of the opposite shore. He imagines that the capital is still covered in mist, smoke, though he can't see it from this side of the island.

Man is mortal, he might as well do something with his life, Andronikos thinks. There's no sense in waiting for death. For years, he had used "love" alongside "death," perhaps without claiming a direct correlation between the two words, but certainly making others think that death was worth loving. But now he suspects he was wrong on this count, too. You must fight death until the very end when death comes towering over you, when, despite your protestations, it carries you away. Only then must you accept death. All these years, as he used beguiling words to argue that those who accumulated wealth, read but a few pages a day, or carried out certain practices simply out of habit were only augmenting their share of mortality, bringing themselves closer to their death, whom had he been trying to frighten, shame or dissuade? Now he's not sure.

He now recognizes that even eating or sleeping, like any other habit, brings one closer to one's death, even praying augments one's share of mortality. The internal rhythm never falters. It has only one stop, only one ending toward which it moves steadily with each passing day. Therefore you must do something new every day, you must recreate, reorder your world anew, each day you must add new dimensions to your life so that you feel as if your share of mortality is diminishing, dissolving, crumbling, so that your life contains something else — and of your own making — beside the modest habits intended to make living easier. Understand, at least prepare yourself to understand that, within this rhythm you are actually living, not merely being swept along.

Andronikos marvels at the lucidity of his mind.

It strikes him as odd that, until today, he has not scrutinized his ideas as much as he is doing now. Drawn into the incredible, the terrifying complacency of faith, he seems to have neglected self-reflection altogether. He also seems to have nursed a stubborn rage in his heart, of the kind that sneers at petty occasions, saving its magnificent eruption for the most opportune moment that never quite arrives, a rage that grows all the keener from endless postponement.

But now the possibility of a life free of rage begins to fill his heart with light. To rid himself of rage, to do something worthwhile. However, while wondering what this worthwhile thing could be, he's still thinking along the predictable lines of growing flowers. He has time to think along different lines, to arrive at a different understanding of worthwhile occupations. There's plenty of time. It doesn't matter to him whether or not others approve of his choice, so long as he averts the sense of futility, impotence.

He returns to impotence again.

Certain concepts have long delineated the limits of his reasoning. Now he can clearly see that his thoughts have continually returned to the idea of impotence, the imperative to do something worthwhile, useful. He should either free himself of this tendency or. . . .

He notices a narrow opening to his right, turns to look. He sees the gravel bank, the rocks, the sea, the prow of his boat. It will be easy to walk down that way. Straight down the trail. He's happy to have found an easy path to the shore. He must stay on the trail.

Asking himself questions, asking questions about himself . . . perhaps self-reflection will be the first thing he'll have learned on the island. Since this morning, he's done everything consciously, deliberately, everything that previously had been or would have been born of habit, performed mechanically. Here he's exercising individual will, what he thought he had been doing as a monk, although he has been taught to deny its existence beyond the confines of his community. He's happy to have learned something new, gained a new intelligence about himself even before his first day on the island is over. He's happy about something else, too: that he doesn't feel the need to disparage this happiness. . . .

He knows the path, he knows the hill, the spring, the shelter he'll build between the rocks. Pleased with himself, he quickens his steps. Happiness tempers his hunger; he knows that walking faster won't tire him right now.

He's descending along what he now recognizes is a dried creek bed. The trees are again left behind. Up ahead, he sees tall rocks, the gravel bank stretching beneath them, he notices a path meandering among the rocks, carved by water.

Like a stairway. Step after step, he descends.

Once he reaches the shore, he's surprised by how easy the descent has been. To his right, the gravel bank leads to a cliff. Near it, he recognizes in the narrow inlet leading into the cave that he entered in the morning. The cliff face isn't tall. His knees still hurt, but even so, it would be easy to climb the cliff, extend his leg across the width of the inlet, then jump to the other side of the gravel bank.

I will never learn, Andronikos chuckles to himself, enjoying the sound of his voice. I will never learn. Why didn't I think of surveying my surroundings before starting my climb this morning?

But he feels pleased with himself — for having taken the difficult path.

It's good to take the difficult path if a person wants to know his character, test his strength, recognize the capacity of his will. Man must start with himself, first steel his being, before he can strive to accomplish anything.

Andronikos stops. By allowing such thoughts to visit his mind, is he doing anything more than idly spinning the wheels of reasoning? Still, to be able to express these thoughts, to order, to shape them into words, to derive strength from these words. . . .

But aren't these new insights the result, the natural consequence of his loss of faith? Aren't they the expressions of a different type of faith, the different faces of a new fixation no less metaphysical than faith? Isn't he merely succumbing to the lure of certain words?

To derive strength from words . . . but unlike the way he did in the past, when he spoke of love or accepted impotence as a given. Perhaps this is the only difference now. Nothing is a given now, nothing a foregone conclusion.

Andronikos wonders: Would it be better if more people thought as he did, if they gave themselves over to similar mind games, braved the risk of self-deception, began to acknowledge possessing extraordinary willpower?

Wouldn't the same reasoning vindicate the Emperor who is ready to defend his decision with fire, who can order the burning of icons, books, houses, people, while knowing precisely the nature, the magnitude of the resistance he'll face?

Andronikos isn't afraid of his thoughts, but he senses that they exceed his limits, the limits of his understanding. At least for the time being, on this first day on the island. . . . Later, he'll have time to weigh these matters. First he'll explore his own limits, determine the exact range of his faculties so that he can force their limits, exceed them. Perhaps he'll succeed; he knows that these limits are not absolute. To widen them, to break through them, ought to be the sole means of human progress. Isn't this the path of greater wisdom, of enlightenment, of knowing God?

The path would probably never end. A person would die first, somewhere along the journey. But if faith is the driving force, if it's faith that urges the person to render his life meaningful, isn't Andronikos hamstrung even before he starts out? Or can something else other than faith inspire man?

Andronikos is hungry.

He straightens his body away from the rock he's been leaning against. He has no time to spend lost in abstractions. He repeats this to himself. Living on this island ought to be different from living at the monastery. He should have thought these matters through at the monastery; it's absurd to do so here. But I wasn't able to, Andronikos thinks, how could I? To seek out his truths at the monastery would have required him to withdraw into the solitude of his cell, even to endure the most arduous rites of penitence. At times, certain tasks can be carried out best in the unlikeliest of places. Secluding himself amidst the crowded community of the monastery would have been a kind of lazy escape, a form of incarceration.

To learn his truths here without withdrawing from life, without resorting to self-incarceration. . . .

He dips his feet in the water. The sea is still perfectly calm, except for the seaweed gently swaying. He becomes conscious of his aching soles, puts on his shoes without tying the laces. Carefully walking on the gravel shore, he reaches his boat. He opens his sack. Cheese, bread, raisins. . . . He ought to ration his food to make it last as long as possible, but today, as hungry as he is, he should perhaps eat a little more than he'll allow himself in the coming days.

Leaning against the rock face, he first tears off a piece of bread, puts it in his mouth, then he eats a pinch of cheese, then a single raisin, another. . . .

Eating slowly, very slowly, Andronikos finishes his meal. He feels the weight of exhaustion in his limbs. He has toiled all night with his arms, all day with his legs. He's not even thinking of the previous day. It occurs to him that he hasn't slept for quite some time.

To climb the hill once again . . . it would be a vain effort.

No one is waiting for him there; neither does he hope or expect to gain anything by climbing. Suffering for the love of God now strikes him as a laughable deception. He listens to the sounds coming from places he can't see — the shrill murmur of the sea on the other side of the island, the rustle of the evergreens above the cliffs. The air is clear, the sky spotless. The sea swells almost imperceptibly. He doesn't expect rain for another day or two. He has plenty of time to build his little hut between the rocks. He doesn't have to climb the hill again tonight. He'll stay here, sleep behind the boat; he'll lay out his sack, his hooded robe on the gravel. Exhausted as he is, he won't feel its rough surface.

Leaning back, he rests his head against the rock. He doesn't want to sleep. He has at least three hours until sunset. Just as his eyes begin to close, he opens them, noticing a shape hovering above him.

The first stork. Ugly. Like a crooked cross. An irregular line extending from the long beak to the tiny head, along the warped neck to the bellows-like body, along the two reedy, straw-like legs — that look like they'll fall off the body any minute — all the way to the tips of spindly claws

— like the fingers of the scraggly stick-figures children draw on walls. Then the two wings, wide, crooked, jutting awkwardly out of the body — like loose, windless sails....

As the stork begins a steep ascent, several other storks emerge from behind the cliff to his right, soaring into the sky. Andronikos realizes: It's the migration season that the children await so excitedly each year, the migration that adults watch with amusement while the elderly, as happy as they are sad for having lived through one more migration, try to interpret the yearly omen that predicts how harsh the winter will be.... The migration of the storks.... Andronikos collects himself.

At present, he is neither a child, nor an adult, nor an elder. He shows no excitement; he doesn't smile. Far from feeling happiness or sorrow, he sees no omens. He simply feels wonder.

The first group of storks that followed after the leader continues its ascent. Andronikos leaps to his feet, jumps across the width of the inlet to the opposite cliff, runs the length of small flat rocks lined up like steps. With all the strength his feet can muster, he rushes toward the top of the precipice, trying to climb a little farther than the rock he'd struggled to reach in the morning. Arriving at a clearing, he tries to determine where the storks are coming from.

Just then he notices legions of storks slowly emerging from the eastern edge of the hill, rising, rising to the sky, flying in his direction. He sits on the ground. The storks continue to multiply, numbering in the hundreds, thousands. In the crimson light of dusk, the dense column of birds radiant with gold, orange flares looks like a bridge extending from the hilltop toward the zenith of the sky. Early in the ascent, some of the stork clusters fly in frenzied disorder, but gradually, they join by instinct the steadily advancing stream. The first stork he saw a while ago is now a speck in the distance.

The earth, the sky, the iridescent bridge between them, endlessly extending, as if intent on spanning the heavens. From time to time, the seagulls' cries mix in with the deafening clatter of the storks. Because they are not leaving, nor do they have any desire to ever leave, the seagulls sound their emphatic notes at the storks, as if boasting about their difference. . . .

Andronikos shouldn't forget that he's not on a Sunday stroll, like an ordinary subject of the venerable Emperor who goes for a swim, wanders among the pines, eats his cheese, bread, raisins, feels tired after having come upon a country-market diversion that God happened to put on his path, returns home, throws his tired body on his bed to quickly fall asleep. Andronikos shouldn't forget. The storks' migration shouldn't make him forget his own migration. Or forget to check whether the city he has left behind is still beset by fires.

At this altitude, he can gaze at the city once again. It's enveloped in mist, but he sees no flames at the moment. Soon the setting sun will drown the city in reddish, coppery, golden hues. Then, even if there is a fire going on in certain quarter, it won't be noticeable. The mist must be concealing the clouds of smoke. It's unlikely that everything condemned to burn has already been burned. The fires can't be stopped until they fulfill their mission. Or could it be that the fires will be set in phases, to brighten the streets with small bonfires every evening, as during festivals? Or perhaps to give the apostates time to reconsider their disobedience? Andronikos acknowledges that his questions will remain unanswered for a long time, as long as he doesn't return to the capital or someone from the capital doesn't come here, bringing him news.

He now inhabits a new world, faces new problems, next to which his old ones will, at least to an extent, lose their significance, their oppressive hold on his mind.

He expects they will.

He saw the flames today but doesn't know what burned. He doesn't know who extinguished the fires, how or why. In fact, he doesn't know whether or not the fires were extinguished.

He expects they were.

He gazes back at the sky, traces the iridescent arc of storks rising from the earth; the flawless motion of sound woven from beating wings is adaptive motion, survival.... A vital task such as this permits no error, disorder or heedless independence. One of the storks up ahead breaks off, begins to fly back toward the earth. Watching with curiosity, Andronikos soon understands why the stork has left the flock: to gather back the few storks straying off the edges. Once the arc is restored, the stork that served as a sheep-dog soars back in exquisite flight, assuming its place in the front.

Andronikos' gaze traces the arc back to the hilltop, notices that it has broken off from the earth. Unexpectedly, he feels distraught, like an incredulous child at a country fair who, at the end of a spectacle he thought would last forever, resists going back home. Andronikos is embarrassed by the feeling. At his age, he ought to be beyond childish disappointments. It's shameful to think otherwise, whether in the city or here, on the island.

Unable to tear his gaze away from the edge of the hill, Andronikos rises to his feet. Just then, a few storks emerge, beginning their ascent through the sky, followed by two more, then, a little later, one last stork, gliding over the water.

Wavering about drowsily in the slanted orange glow of the setting sun, this particular stork is like the heedless youth who, after carousing until dawn, arises from sleep much too late, then rushes out of the house without even washing his face, anxious to catch up with his merry accomplices. All of a sudden, an outrider stork, another sheep-dog, breaks off from the flock, rushing back at lightning speed to peck at the errant bird. At first, the lone stork attempts to put up resistance, to defend himself against the disciplinarian beak, but soon, duly admonished, hurries to catch up with the other tardy birds that had somehow managed to take wing a few seconds ahead of him. Even after this last batch of storks joins the floating arc, the sheep-dog does not relent. First, he flies toward the edge of the hill, hovers above it as if to make sure that no one is left behind. Then, he turns around, flies back, but slowly, intently, as if scanning the rocks, the hollows, the surface of the sea for more errant birds. Finally convinced that all his charges are accounted for, he races forth like an arrow shot from a marksman's bow. Silence returns to the hill. The seagulls are quiet, the clattering storks inaudibly distant.

Andronikos leaves his watching post, returns to the shore, filled with the melancholy of autumn, of leave-taking. The storks' migration, the vigilant sheep-dog, the lazy or, who knows, perhaps unwilling, defiant birds, their last revolt — these he ought to consider tomorrow. For now, he needs to clear his mind, purge it of the tendency to embellish or interpret experiences; he wants to focus only on the purity of images.

The cliffs outlining the shore leading to the cave cast long shadows. . . . The pale, cold light seems to dissipate gradually. A boat with rose-hued sails enters his field of vision, floating toward the city. Perhaps it will manage to drop anchor before nightfall.

Andronikos recognizes the boat that carried him to Chalcedon yesterday. He imagines the passengers aren't yet aware of what is happening in the city. True, for two days, while the inhabitants had been anticipating what was to come, they had remained quiet until the Emperor's edict was announced. Although Andronikos was merely traveling to Chalcedon — there was nothing strange or unusual about someone, even a monk, traveling to Chalcedon — he'd felt the need to fabricate all kinds of excuses when talking to the boat's captain. Ashamed, embarrassed, he'd reproached himself for sinking deep into the quicksand of deception. Now the same sailboat was returning to the reality of the city.

Andronikos thinks he's probably safe for now, but regrets that his lies lost him the opportunity to be a brave fugitive or a hero in the eyes of the boat captain. No, he corrects himself: Being known as a fugitive should be enough. It's the only accurate description of who he is. Neither bravery nor heroism has anything to do with him. Yet Andronikos does sense his desire to exaggerate his character. Is it because exhaustion makes a person feel his insignificance all the more keenly that he succumbs to self-aggrandizement, trying to fool himself with illusions of greatness?

He opens his eyes after what must have been quite a long nap, since his surroundings have grown considerably darker. He should bring this day to a close, finish it off, in order to gather strength for tomorrow. He has much to do, even though he hasn't figured out what or how. Let that be tomorrow's task.

He walks to the water's edge, washes his hands, splashes his face. He then kneels on the ground to recite his evening prayer, half awake half asleep. Raising his head at the end of his prayer, he notices distant flecks of light sliding on the sea surface. Fishermen from the village on the opposite shore, he thinks. If they come nearer, they might see me, if they find me agreeable enough, perhaps I can join them, become a fisherman.

The brashness of his idea frightens Andronikos; at the same time, to rid his mind of an idea just because it's frightening strikes him as cowardly. In any case, it's a premature idea. Shouldn't the fishermen first decide whether they want to take him along? Would they even come to the island?

Regardless of whether they would or not, he should first build his shelter. It should be his first task tomorrow. Maybe finding stones won't be as easy as he imagined. Suddenly, stretching before him — slightly above sea level on the southwest slope of the hill — are the ruins of the palace where, a quarter century earlier, the Empress had entertained hoards of noble courtiers. In the garden behind the palace, hundreds of trees are loaded with plums, cherries, pears, apples. Radiant with ripe colors but wild from neglect, the trees calmly sway to the rhythm of the wind, as if proud to bear the weight of so many fruits. Andronikos can eat some, curb his hunger, he can also dry some to store for winter. Only one thing surprises him: that all these fruits — the plums, the apples, the cherries, the pears — grow side by side. . . .

Once he decides he should benefit from this abundance, why shouldn't he help himself to the stones of the palace ruins in order to build his little dwelling between the rocks that he spotted near the stream on the hill?

The idea pleases him. It would be inappropriate to dwell among the ruins of a palace. He would feel small, dwarfed by the shadows of lost grandeur, but he can certainly use the stones. If only his heart can accept that he isn't brave, that he doesn't wish to be brave. . . .

In front of him stands the mast of a boat. Andronikos starts in panic. The fishermen must have arrived.

But he's lying on the ground, his hands, tucked under his head, press against the gravel. . . . The mast in front of him belongs to his boat. He tries to figure out when his dream began, when it ended. He tries to shake off sleep. The palace, the plums, the apples, the cherries, the pears, all of these belong to his dream. On the drowsy edges of wakefulness is the struggle to convince his heart that he is not brave. . . .

Tomorrow he'll search for the palace ruins. God may have sent him the vision. Does he want to believe that God would still send him visions? Why not? God isn't stingy. . . . Andronikos will look for the ruins. If he can't find them, then he'll break stones with his hands, carry them up the hill. He must recover his strength for the task, he must sleep, he mustn't give in to helplessness.

To love, to create, to build — not in words, but in deeds. These impulses ought to be lived.

Andronikos struggles to lift his body, get on his feet, to avoid dozing off again. He walks to the back of the boat, lays his sack on a rock so he can rest his head against it. It's warm here. The gravel, the stones are warm. Wrapping himself in his robe, he pulls his knees to his chest, tucks his feet into the folds of his robe. The ground is hard but he has to get used to it. He closes his eyes. This time knowing, feeling, sensing what he's doing.

But he's unable to sleep, as if swimming in a liquid state of wakefulness. Slowly, very slowly, he extends his legs. I am alone, he says, alone, alone. . . . He hears the words reverberate throughout his being, but they sound as if the voice speaking them is not his. He turns, lies on his belly, but feels that he must do something more. He presses his chest against the gravel. Harder, harder. Until his flesh almost feels indistinguishable from the gravel. His voice reaches his ears: My God! Do I believe in you? Do I even believe in you?

His fingers tighten, his hands close around the stones, squeeze until they hurt. Feeling his aching hipbones pressed against the gravel, he thinks of Ioakim.

1963

73

HILL

Rainy or cold, evening after evening for years, he has been doing one thing, his palms damp with cool sweat each time, his hands tingling, his whole being trembling with excitement, as if each evening is the first time he's leaning on his staff, dragging his tired feet, climbing the foothill of Aventius.

But it seems that the days when he had to trust his staff more than his feet, even those days are behind him now. His staff is still firm, but nowadays he can't trust his arms or the hands that grip his staff. With November coming to an end, he knows the sunny evenings are numbered. For a few weeks now, when he sits under the solitary poplar on the riverbank during the drowsy afternoon hours, he's noticed the rushing water is closer to brown than green, dead leaves, broken branches, rotting baskets swirl in the eddies, while a dense muddy current runs down the middle of the riverbed; a few days ago, the waters had swept along the carcass of a dog. . . .

All these signal that, far away in the higher provinces, winter has begun, bringing with it the heavy rains. Almost no one from the northern cities visits anymore. Those places might even be covered with snow by now. Here it rains from time to time, while the weather gradually gets colder. But even if the month of December remains sunny, he'll have to wait until March for the sun to warm his aching bones, soothe them again. No matter how seldom it might rain, the soil will stay damp, the stones cold until March.

To see March again, to feel the warm sun in his joints, to watch the river gradually change from brown to green, to taste again the watermelon, the fig, the grape — these seem to him now as incredible, as improbable as fairy tales from faraway times, faraway places, vaguely remembered. Yet is it not also true that tasting the fig, the grape once again will bring him closer to another winter, sweep him into an altogether incredible, all the more improbable adventure? Will he not experience all the more keenly in his heart that being ever near is also being never, ever there?

This evening he will again turn his back to the river, to the roaring currents; walking to the right of his little hut — his castle, his palace, his temple in this city where he neither was born nor grew up, but where he will most certainly die, in the soil of which he will be buried — he'll reach the fork in the road, then take the path to the right. One more time. He won't walk; rather, he'll drag his feet behind his staff as he has done most every evening lately; prayerfully, he'll repeat to himself, I am not descending to the valley but climbing up the hill; he'll try to keep up with the sun, aware that, each day, he has to start out a little earlier; trying in vain to quicken his steps while feeling in his heart the futility of exertion, he will climb the foothill of Aventius.

Toward the edge of the woods.

He feels his seventy years on this earth in his every step. These days, he's often visited by the memory — distant, very distant, though it still feels like yesterday — of the seventy-year-old monk in the monastery he had entered when he was but a downy-cheeked boy. That old man had a self-possessed vitality about him. His walk was quicker, more agile, his back straighter, his sight sharper than his own are now. That's how he remembers it. . . .

The only part of his body that showed his age were his ears. He remembers being told when he first arrived at the monastery that the old monk had been deaf for nearly twenty years. Back then, twenty years seemed to him as unimaginable as the world that lay beyond the city walls. He had not even turned eighteen. The seventy-year-old monk had seemed as though he'd forgotten the umbilical cord — long since torn, shriveled — that tied him to the world of sounds; he had stopped listening or reading lips to figure out what was being said; speaking sparingly, only to say what was most essential, he spent his days reading, praying, walking around the courtyard — his eyes fixed on his feet — losing himself in contemplation. . . . One day in the courtyard

And in those early days, was he getting to know Andronikos? He must have spoken to him, at least asked him a question, perhaps even on his first day at the monastery. But he must have been timid; he vaguely remembers that Andronikos hadn't shown much interest in him. Despite his own natural unease about opening up to people, perhaps he'd felt an affinity toward Andronikos, finding him to be more thoughtful than others, more

It's none of this. When someone begins to think of past events from the perspective of fairy tales he's prone to invent from subsequent events — fairy tales that increasingly resist any resemblance to reality — and when he in turn begins to interpret subsequent events in light of those fairy tales

Yet, that old age makes us keenly aware of these inventions, that reality occupies such a small space in human lives, that we agree willingly to allow it such a small space

Andronikos was perhaps the first person he felt close to. Eventually. The first person he wanted to speak with, the first he spoke with, the first he began loving, the first he trusted, depended on

The first who would hurt him, the first who would make him taste disappointment, the one who would later teach him the biggest lesson of his life. Still, that old monk

Still, that monk, how unconventional he was

Still, that monk, always held by, always held by conventions

One day, while waiting timidly in the courtyard, he had raised his head, looked up. The old monk was walking toward him, though as if he hadn't noticed him. Ioakim had stepped aside, leaned against a column. The monk stopped right in front of him. Even now Ioakim can feel the chill of the column between his shoulder blades. . . . The monk acted as if he had somehow noticed the boy standing like a stone figure, staring at him half in fear half in admiration. Looking straight at him, the monk had extended his withered hand, squeezed the boy's chin, caressed his cheek with the back of his hand. Ioakim remembers first noticing the old monk's beard quivering, but he hadn't immediately understood that he was about to speak. Then, a faint, whistle-like voice — Ioakim couldn't be certain where it was coming from — had spoken: "Good boy, lovely boy." Then, the beard no longer quivering, the mouth had opened further, emitting a much louder, cracked yet firm voice: "Wish you were already as deaf as I am. . . ." Never again did the seventy-year-old monk speak to him, acting not even as if he'd forgotten Ioakim, but as if he had never taken notice of the boy in the first place. Nevertheless, in every encounter after that, Ioakim would slowly bow his head, feeling the need to greet him.

Shortly before winter that year, the old monk had withdrawn to his cell for a penitential fast; on the morning of the eighth day, the news of his death had spread among the community. His dead body had seemed taller, younger to Ioakim.

Why remember these things now?

Then, always mixed in with these memories, was the fox. The kit fox tied to the base of a column with a slender chain, leaping around with the half-ease its long chain offered, delighting in playing with everyone who showed it love, nipping then leaping back, nipping then leaping back, a game it favored over any other game....

But what did the old man and the little fox have in common? What do they have in common at this present moment?

He feels a burning sensation in his hands so tightly gripping his staff, a sticky dampness in his palms. A shiver runs through his body underneath the heavy folds of his coarse woolen robe.

He feels something like queasiness, like the queasiness of fear, like the queasiness of a fear-stricken heart: that old taste of his failings, his guilt, slowly rising from his stomach to his mouth. As if it has hounded him all his life. As if he has known the sensation since birth, therefore grown accustomed to it, in the way someone grows accustomed to a diseased stomach, a crippled leg, a blind eye, feeling the occasional pain, the pain of his failings, his affliction, his brokenness.... This taste, this familiar taste that still visits him from time to time

He stops. There is no point in even thinking about it. He has only one choice: to experience this painful, burning, bilious taste of failings, brokenness, guilt, slowly rising to his mouth, to wait, to endure, silently.

This is all he feels, nothing else.

On account of the little animal. The kit fox tied with a slender chain to the base of a column, in the monastery courtyard.

But not just on account of the animal. Or is it enough to know that much?

That he asks, that he feels he must ask this particular

question, does it not seem to complete a missing piece of his evening excursions, of this ritual of his?

But how were the two linked?

He is truly shivering. But not because of the cold air.

It's the coldness of the soil, he says to himself. Of the soil heaping up inside him with each passing day — the coldness of imminent death, his share of mortality. How often it visits me lately, he says, even this very moment, even at moments like this. Perhaps it's my turn to withdraw to my cell for my last penance.

But he thinks he has no right. He knows he has not yet earned the right to such a manner of dying.

Certainly not this evening of exceptional harmony, blessed calm; to regurgitate the past, to persist so stubbornly, despite his age. . . .

He ought to feel shame, nothing else.

The evening is beautiful, the air soft. Yet he feels this cold soil, this cold water, coursing through his bones, his flesh, the surface of his skin; were it not for this inner chill, he could even say that the air is warm. In reality, none of this accounts for the beauty, the singular beauty of the evening. He has to find another word, different words, to describe how he is feeling.

Something is born, it grows out of the air's softness. When he started his walk, there was sunlight, but also a cool breeze beginning to make itself felt. Now, after walking for some time, after experiencing the light drunkenness of exhaustion in his joints, his flesh, after bearing all the burden of exertion in his arms, his legs, he isn't surprised that a wave of heat begins to seep through his skin, to the interior of his body. The inner chill shooting outward like crackling sparks is also a sensation he has known for a long time. But as the sun retreats behind Mount Aventius, the shadows deepen along the path he's been walking, the rustling grows louder, sharper, among the leaves, among the branches — somewhat sparse yet still green — in the woods ahead of him, as the soft, diffuse light swells then redoubles. Ioakim thinks of a thick nectar, how, suspended in that liquid, the faded, translucent petals of a rose suddenly become something beyond roseness, beyond petalness, beyond pure sweetness. Dense, ripening — this, the word he's been looking for — one

Ripening. He is thinking of fruit now, ripening fruits, their skin growing thinner, breaking open, as if they can no longer remain hidden, covered, no longer contain the softness, the sweetness teeming inside of them. . . . The edges of the split skin blacken quickly. Within days, within hours, the onset of death — call it rot, call it mold, call it blackness. Is it not also true that what protects the rose petals, what carries them beyond roseness, petalness, sweetness, is exactly their half-dissolution in the nectar?

The air has a color. A diffuse color, the inexhaustible, irrepressible, changeless color of Rome. One that, in a way, reminds him of the color of his own country, his own city, Byzantium, that has banished him. But different from that color.

To his left is the immense arena — now no more than a desolate, abandoned ditch — that once echoed with shouts, cheers, screams of pain, screams of jubilation, jeers, applause. It seems caught in sleep, a swampy, muddy, reed-filled, infested sleep. Would the Hippodrome in Byzantium become like this someday? Are hundreds, thousands of people still gathered there? Are they still rushing to play or watch others play the bloody games? In all likelihood, this vast swamp, this immense arena designed for galloping horses, was once upon a time as much alive as Byzantium's Hippodrome. Now it is dead. Old Rome long gone, having left behind one unforgettable color — if you don't count the jaundiced, ashen, mossy, glum whiteness of the marbles still standing here, there

The color of red brick

Would Byzantium also disappear someday? New Rome, sovereign, thriving in the middle of these boundless lands, as if she has inherited the glory of Old Rome, who would sack her one day? Who can, who, coming where from, can pillage that other Rome as they did this Rome? Even the thought of it is inconceivable, is it not?

It is not. . . . Why should it be? Was this Rome not sacked, burned?

Those gathered in the grand arena to watch the games, do they still provoke fights, try to kill one another? Or are the games banned now?

Byzantine bricks are of two colors, rough cut. But the dominant color that extends beyond the color of the walls in Byzantium — the blue, green lilac, lead color of the sea — is absent here. After the games at the Hippodrome, the people who spilled out onto the streets would, by tilting their heads ever so slightly, come upon that color, which enveloped the entire city. Yet the spectators leaving this arena, if they were to gaze westward between the hills, they may or may not have seen the waters of the river

This is what Rome lacks: the omnipresent color of the sea. Rome must make do with the blue of the sky.

To exhaust something, anything, one must use it

To exhaust life

That, too. To exhaust it, you must first begin

To treat life like a holy feast day that might never arrive, like

Perhaps by following this reasoning, he will arrive at something

Just as you prepare for a holy feast day, just as all of life's labor, its worries are validated, justified with the arrival of the holy feast day

That is, if the holy feast day arrives

He stops here. The holy feast, if it arrives. . . .

Yet, if an entire life is spent in preparation for the holy feast day that doesn't arrive. . . .

How often in his life did he find himself saying, "It's here"? How often did the holy feast day actually arrive, with it

Even now. Can he be certain that the holy feast ever arrived?

He is dwelling on an image

But as soon as he calls it an image, as soon as his mind calls it forth, the idea it represents takes the form of a vow. This vow. This vow — whether or not he has succeeded in keeping it — has it not given direction to his life? Has this vow not guided his entire life?

Has he not done everything for the sake of this vow? At the least, does it not appear to be so? He ought to be able to renounce the vow, too. Here, that vow has to have no meaning, no value, beyond the one it once held, when it used to guide his life. But not here, certainly not now. Every vow bears a distinct reality, a distinct value, in a given place, a given time

Yet to dwell on the myriad particularities of an image, a painting, colors set side by side, or even one color, all this is futile thinking. Should he not renounce especially this numbing habit?

There is a faint, distant buzzing in the air. Like a woman wailing beside her dead child, stringing her laments one after another, her voice coiling along the links of her long chain of laments. A faint buzzing, rising then receding to the rhythm of the breeze. It must be coming from the reeds, the mosquitoes swarming the reed beds. He is thinking of the sallow-faced children with distended bellies who live in the huts along the fallen walls that lie across the wide swamp cradled by hills, far away from the city, in a distance measured on horseback. But this lament is coming not from the mothers of those children but from the mosquitoes.

With the help of his staff, he straightens his body again. How often he must nowadays, he's lost count. Just a few years ago, he would straighten his body once when reaching the woods, maybe three more times afterwards. But now

In the past, he would not have looked to his left until he made it to the woods. He would have avoided looking in that direction with the resolve of a person who knew all too well what he would see, the sense of awe he would eventually experience upon seeing it. If his head or eyes were to slant to the left, ever so slightly, he would abruptly look away from the view. Back in those days, this joy of postponement — ever greater as he resisted looking — this joy, this sense of awe, he would have released like a ball, like a dove, like a shot released from his hands, from his ribcage, from the sling of his eyes, flung it forth, toward the mouths caught in a centuries-long yawn.

But now, each time he straightens his body, a shiver courses through his being, the icy breeze claws at the back of his neck, he tenses his frame a little more, draws his neck in a little more, glances ahead; each glance, he knows, is added to the previous glances, each serving as an advance on the future, increasing the joy that awaits him at the end of his path. He derives pleasure from the avarice of hoarding each glance, experiencing each time even greater terror, fearing an even greater loss.

There, at the woods' edge, he will be the ball, the dove, the shot once again.

He will be the kit fox.

In the ripe air, in the ripe light of the evening — that tastes like a ripe fruit, its skin already starting to split open — inside this calm, translucent air, he will be like the kit fox.

He squints, creases his eyelids, squeezing them shut.

He can't understand how he mustered the courage to

ask — even if while feeling shame, even if he's only asking himself — about the nature of the link between them.

That morning when he watched from his cell's window the dark-haired, dark-cloaked, dark-mustachioed, beardless wretch with the dark countenance hounding the little fox that struggled to escape as far as the chain around its neck allowed (already tormented by the children's voices, the animal was no longer able to — or pretended not to — notice their laughter, the stones hurled at it, or the blood running down its thigh), frantically thrusting its nose against a wall, when he watched them that morning, did he feel pity along with anger, he didn't know, but could he have imagined even as recently as yesterday that he would dig up the roots of his shame today — in this moment, in this place separated from the past by seas, mountains, cities, countries — by remembering the moment when he rushed out of his cell, stunned the man with his youthful outrage, the power of his sacred robe, grabbed the kit fox in his arms, then slammed the door shut on the man's dark countenance?

One more step. Is he not going to think of all this when he lies in his bed tonight? But he has long given up making these nightly inventories of his day, weighing his acts against his thoughts, his feelings against his obligations, deriving from these certain guidance, certain maxims to use in the days ahead so as to live a better, more obedient life that would please God, honor His commandments; it has been so very long since he stopped believing that he could fulfill this longing. Now, when he lies in his bed, little else than old, displaced memories visit his mind, the chambers beneath his eyelids.

Until that day, he had not witnessed the agony of a person or an animal. He hadn't yet seen the face of a man dying in agony, dying of agony. He knew some who died quickly, in a matter of minutes, he had seen them once. Those who did not know what was happening to them, whose astonishment bore the form of a disbelief that must have lasted beyond their death. . . . He also knew their loved ones, how they struggled with the thoughts swarming their minds, the actuality of fate. He knew the piercing gaze of the dead, their eyes, before they were closed. But one dying of agony . . . until that day

When?

He had experienced the fear of dying of agony on that day.

When was that? Which day?

Those who flailed themselves beside their dead, he knew their thoughts, their insidiously twisting, writhing, wrangled thoughts beneath their pain. How would they eat, who would pay for the funeral, how would they live without support, without a wife, a child, a mother, a sibling . . . these were the questions; then there were the secret joys felt on account of the death, the secret satisfaction that God had taken upon Himself the burden of an overdue revenge. . . . Though on that day, when Ioakim witnessed for the first time one dying of agony

Of course he knows now when it was

Worse still, this agony had not been the agony of pulled fingernails, gouged eyes, slit noses, sliced tongues, pulled teeth, crushed bones or dismemberment. The most horrific of agonies, the most unrelenting, the most maddening

The kind that overwhelmed the minds of bystanders, onlookers, listeners, leaving no room for any other thought

On that day when he had tasted the fear of dying of agony, he had made his decision.

He had decided on that day but had to wait for nearly fifteen years before he could, here

Now, as he is doing what he has done every evening

for years, each time as if for the first time, his whole being trembling, his palms wet with the icy cold sweat of excitement, every evening, in rain or cold, now, as he is climbing the foothill of Aventius — leaning on his staff, his tired footsteps weighed down by the day's burden, by years of guilt — he's actually remembering those other walks he used to take, every evening for nearly a year, before setting out for Rome.

Just as no one knows exactly where the sun rises or where it sets, conversely, just as everyone knows with reasonable certainty the path the sun follows during the day, just as this sun hanging above you at the noon hour is among the few things you know with absolute certainty in this world, so do the farthest reaches of the walk vanish into the misty forgottenness of a certain fog-covered meadow, while near the midpoint, the summit, the noon hour, the brightest moment of the walk, memories gradually come into light, then, once at the summit — the walker caught in the acute brilliance of a piece of ice that refuses to thaw, beholding the point where the arms of the sea converge — the walk attains a kind of eternity that defies all other memories.

It would be wrong to say that he wasn't thinking of anything in particular while climbing. Perhaps he didn't have a particular thought in his mind, but perhaps he transcended thought, transcended consciousness, to the extent that he wouldn't even have noticed that he was thinking the same thing, or the same two or three things. He realized this possibility now, when he attempted to recapture, to relive, that particular walk from the past. Much later, like others his age, he, too, would come to recognize that nothing can be relived after so many years, that he had to accept each walk as a new event, as a new way of being. He'd thought of nothing when starting out. Except for the beauty he would encounter at the top of the hill.

Only months later did it occur to him one evening that his climbs recalled another walk, that they served as a symbol of another path, now in the distant past.

Another path with indefinite beginning, indefinite ending. A path made of, extended by, everyday experiences. But at one point along this path, the walker would arrive at such a summit that everything becomes clearly visible, unimpeded by shadows, bathed in brilliant light. The sea's three arms coming together in a knot before his eyes — whatever associations the scene may have evoked were immaterial — signaled a union, a kind of exaltation. He was now able to see, to know, the full beauty of his native city.

A steadily emptying form among the different colors, the different lights of different evenings

The experience was similar to discovering that an ornate box once full to the brim had been emptied out one day, realizing that you never knew its contents — you still didn't — that it had been emptied out without your noticing. Left behind were only the familiar engravings on the box, which alone interested you; your eyes, your hands, your heart sought nothing else, instead settled for these few particulars accentuated by familiarity

This steadily emptying form, this walk that gradually became the shadow of something beautiful, this walk that resembled living, crowned by a moment of fullness, of completeness, experienced at the summit while gazing at one's surroundings, at the past, at the ordeal of the long ascent, the moment of rest before the descent, the soon-to-begin descent toward death, the moment of equilibrium that gained meaning because recognizing it demanded every ounce of one's strength, this walk that, in time, began to feel like a sorrowful recess, a heart-rending remorse, a thorn in the side of one's commonplace life.

His was the pain of still being alive, of having long

delayed a decision, and, even after making it, of having done nothing other than taking these evening excursions. He had been willing to endure this pain, this thorn that had become as familiar as a habit.

All his anguish, regrets, feelings of guilt, concentrated in this thorn, now no more than an empty abstraction, a mental image; he took refuge in its pain to avoid thinking of the rest; enduring this pain willingly because it was his refuge actually worsened it, which in turn allowed him to forgive himself, if to a small degree; his willingness to forgive himself in turn denigrated him in his own eyes, which in turn obtained him a certain amount of happiness that he tried to pretend he didn't feel. He was caught in this unrelenting circle — not even futile, it was like the mindless circling of a horse yoked to the water-mill that disallowed even thinking of futility. Worse still, the mill-horse helped to irrigate the fields, whereas he was throwing sand at the desert surrounding him. All of this had become clear to him when

He had finally set out on the path.

That was also when he had begun the task of exhausting life, as he called it. But only superficially, without mining the depths, meticulously avoiding the depths

But today, as he revisits these thoughts, he's trying to make sense of them, to sort out the contents of his mind earnestly, without getting caught up in the childish pretenses that he once took for introspection.

He has to stop. Not his thoughts, but this drifting away. He must reacquaint himself with light, air, heat, sweat, exhaustion, the chill that runs through his body, the path to the summit, his staff, the trees, the tree line

The tree line, the color of the stream flowing beyond it, this particular evening, his bed, images coming alive, beginning to fill the dome above his head, the enclosed, roofed heavens with their still luminescence, images that construe for him the ever-growing meaning of his homeland

He must gather them back to his mind.

He must stop at once, this last — the newest — of his elusions . . . how many thousands of them, he has lost count.

He takes deep labored breaths. His eyes are closed. If they weren't, the world would seem shrouded in darkness. His queasiness begins to feel like that desire to faint felt in moments of increased exhaustion, of deepened melancholy. He slowly opens his eyes, looks to his left, below him, at what was once an arena, now covered with rushes that remember neither the crowds nor the horses. Above the rushes are swirling clouds of tiny insects. He does not yet look at the opposite shore.

He tries to straighten his body. Tonight the path before him seems to stretch farther. Now there are trees on both sides. What he remembers as the woods is still a ways off. Little by little, Aventinus's shadow is advancing toward the path. Soon he'll be walking in the shade; when he reaches the woods, the tree line, the rushes, too, will be enveloped in this shadow. Then, only the opposite shore, only those ancient walls, the immense mouths that have been yawning for centuries will be swimming in light.

What Andronikos did, was it heroic? Was Andronikos a hero?

For years — nearly an entire lifetime — he has been grappling with this question, endlessly turning it over in his mind but never bringing himself to answer it. No, that's not quite correct. He's reluctant to think about the meaning of heroism, that is, reluctant to define it, that is, to admit to himself that he must first define it, that is, once he defines it, to feel obligated to consider the value of heroism in light of that definition.

His belief that he must stop, stop all forms of elusion,

does it not have to do with, among other things, his recognition of his reluctance?

I will probably die soon, he thinks to himself. If I were not dying, why would I behave as if I have to figure out everything tonight, as if I must assign definite meanings to certain acts, to certain deeds from years past?

He will not die

Because his behavior belies that possibility.

If only death were as easy as this. But it's difficult. He knows the difficulty of death. Man endlessly bears the weight of his wrongs, his sins. Worse still, he learns at a very early age that neither other people nor God would forgive these wrongs, these sins, yet only much later does he start believing what he learned, accepting what he learned. He doesn't die. He can't die. His weight crushes him because he is ashamed.

Because he is powerless.

His eyes are again closed while he utters these words.

He takes a step, then another step.

Is he finally arriving at the summit of the path he has been walking all his life? Is today the day when he will reach the summit, when he will stand not at Byzantium's acropolis but on the foothill of Aventinus, behold not the three arms of the sea winding into a knot, but the ages of Rome, from past to future, its time everlasting? If he arrives at that summit today, if he reaches that bright light, just as one feels jubilant while approaching the sea after having walked or ridden on horseback for countless hours, countless days, just as one arrives at the open shore of the open sea by galloping past the last range of hills, the row of hedges, the brush, just as one, upon arriving, has to either dive into that sea, wade, swim away, disappear, or return, just as one, after having seen the sea, drawn its salt into one's lungs, returns without any desire to look back, walks the same path back while knowing full well that it will lead to no place, absolutely nowhere, Ioakim also will have to return from that summit, return without the chance of reaching it ever again. He knows this: He will return little by little, like falling asleep, like descending into death — although, compared with the pace of the ascent that has lasted an entire lifetime, the return will feel like a frenzied tumble — he'll return to his cell, cloister himself, never to emerge. He knows this because he has learned it well over the years. If nothing else, this is probably the one benefit of a long life, he says to himself.

Cloister himself in his cell, no longer thinking of the kit fox

No longer imagining the day when, suddenly appearing before an eighteen-year-old neophyte, a monk's apprentice, he might have extended his fingers to touch his chin

Without thinking that nothing is wrong with him, that the other monks would find his penitential retreat strange

He'll cloister himself.

Thinking about, in a way, beginning to live, then, having begun, about ending life, exhausting it, by beginning, by ending

What Andronikos had done was heroic.

Not just at the end, he had acted heroically all along.

Beginning with his escape.

No, this will not do.

Once again he finds himself on the ice-covered slope from a time past, the slope outside a childhood home at the top of a hill, the steep, glass-like surface, made so by the neighborhood children sliding, sliding down; he finds himself experiencing the same feeling of effortlessness as when he used to step out the door of his home, begin sliding down, without the least exertion.

Around here, he's told, it snows once every forty years.

He feels as if he's been walking for hours. But the shade has spread just enough to cover his path, spilling over only in places. One could say he has been walking not for hours but for years. Ever since those days many years ago when, stepping out the door of his hilltop home, he would let his body slide effortlessly down the slope, the steep, glass-like surface made by the children sliding downhill. The only annoyance he had to suffer was the climb back up, holding onto walls, advancing slowly, taking step after cautious step to avoid tripping or falling on his face, so he could reach his front door once again, once again let himself slide down at full speed.

Now, too, he is trying to slide down a steep slope.

Yet, around here, he is told, it snows once every forty years.

He's too old to let his body slide down, then climb back. That's why now he's climbing first, then descending.

He's still escaping, still finding the way to escape.

As for Andronikos, his heroism had started with his escape.

Refusing to flaunt the courage of a person who rejects defeat, he had joined the heroes' ranks by escaping.

Much later, he had heard from Andronikos himself the story of this escape, of his arrival on the island. That one day he would call him a hero on account of this escape

Even though he disparaged his own escape

Was it because he loved Andronikos that

For the longest time, he had considered heroism as something neither exalted nor exalting but crude, degrading

No, not degrading

He simply sees it as neither exalted nor exalting.

Grapes grow in certain soil, bluefish live in certain waters, so are heroes created in certain cities, certain human communities. It makes no difference that he recoiled from any type of heroism himself, or that he resisted the label of hero with all his strength. What matters is for those cities, for those human communities that once raised heroes to be altered, to the point that they no longer raise heroes. That they no longer need to raise heroes. How or when such a change might occur? No one knows yet.

Not just those who escaped the way Andronikos had, even those who escaped the way Ioakim had, are they not thought of as some kind of heroes around here? True, the intervening thirty years have managed to dispense with heroism of any kind, blotted out all notions, all memories of heroism, even the traces of those memories. But words still carry meaning, significance. Those — words, their meanings — do not die as easily.

Like the kit fox.

Thrashing about under water, unable to shake off the hand that held it under water, the little fox that refused to drown.

While holding that fox under the water inside that tub, inside that stone, coffin-shaped pool, he had tried to extinguish the last spark of desire to become a hero in his heart, to make sure no one would deign to call him a hero.

He's angry that he hadn't recognized his motive with such ease, such clarity then, as he does now. Is his anger not a sign of childishness, perhaps senility?

But he resists accepting either childishness or senility. He won't tolerate them. He takes one more step, one more step, feeling it deeply in his being.

The shadows have deepened further, gnawing at the reed beds along the edges of the swamp that no longer remembers the fall of ancient charioteers.

On the opposite side, mouths held open for centuries, slowly, slowly

Like a corpse, its flesh decomposing for centuries, intestines, spleen, entrails, now mud clumps, bared, visible

Like a realization, sudden, that certain words, idioms, assumed to have lost their meaning after so much repetition, had, at least some time in the past, actually carried discrete meanings

The recesses underneath the arches bearing the ceilings, the walls, the recesses in which people once dwelled, lived, lived, dwelled, experienced all things conceivable, inconceivable, these recesses that now resemble toothless mouths are slowly, slowly painted in the richest of colors, the color of earth, as they receive the rays of the sun setting across from them.

And while those mouths — helplessly caught in their yawning — gradually take on the color of earth, that warm, full, most beautiful color of death that lies beyond a life lived with abandon, a life exhausted fearlessly, are they not also harboring the promise of some sort of immortality as they stare at the dying day, as if certain that light will return at the end of darkness? Since that day when death, the most solemn of all feasts, came to rip open the outer walls, exposing the hollow interiors of these mouths.

Will he suddenly understand today — or at least find in him the wherewithal to understand — those men who are never sober, whose bodies have long since ceased to seek any sustenance other than wine, because they are not reluctant, not afraid, to live out, exhaust, their lives in destitution?

I will not be able to finish this sentence, he says to himself. I will get to weave this sentence together, finish it, only when I reach the summit to see that those yawning mouths are warmed by the setting sun, in the final light of the dying day. It will be my last utterance. Until then

Suddenly, he's surrounded by children. Laughing, screaming, growling, howling children. Savage, as always, as everywhere. He freezes. Reacts too late. One of them even dares to grab his staff, pull it away, Ioakim straightens himself. The children fall back, but, seeing that his staff remains on the ground, they decide not to run away, instead keep him surrounded. One shouts at him, Crazy! Another shouts, Stranger! A third follows suit, screaming, Crazy Stranger! He talks to himself, says another. Shame on you, says another, are you not ashamed?

Ioakim is of course ashamed, but the child had not addressed his question to him.

He grabs his staff, clutching his two hands around it, brings it down as if stabbing the ground, moves a step, lifts the staff, then brings it down again. So he will have to walk like this for a while. Unexpectedly, the children quiet down; in the silence, a woman's voice is heard from beyond the woods, calling a boy then a girl, or rather, a male name then a female name. All of the children run toward the voice. They know they're being called to supper, Ioakim thinks, of course they'll run.

He forgets the children. Exerts more effort now. To climb, to move forward. He must have little time left. How many years since he started on the path? He has been walking for maybe ten minutes, maybe less.

The kit fox hadn't run or skipped but rather it would leap from one column to the next. He had placed a big bowl in front of the animal, which he'd filled with moistened pieces of bread mixed with scraps. To get the bowl from his cell, the bread, the scraps from the kitchen, he'd tied the animal to the base of a column. But the little fox, curled into a ball between two columns, wasn't going to budge. In all likelihood, the animal knew that it was saved from the man's punishing hand, from the children's pokers, their kicks, their roaring laughter, or that it was spared the senselessness of trying to press its muzzle against a wall or endlessly sniffing around the base of them, but that was the extent of its knowledge. The animal would not even tilt its head back to lick its wound.

But in the days that followed, the kit fox had managed to heal its wound, even learned to play without tugging at the long, slender chain that Ioakim had tied around its neck instead of the rope. One by one, the animal had devised sundry games all by itself — hand-biting, chasing, hide-and-seek. At first, the other monks had said nothing to Ioakim, viewing his interest in the animal as a youthful fancy. But a few weeks later, when the little fox's tail regained its fullness, its shiny whiskers began curving like bows just the way a healthy animal's would, some of the monks had changed their attitude, some arguing that this childish fancy was dragging out too long, others beginning to wonder whether Ioakim would ever dedicate himself to religion or preferred instead tending to animals that belonged in the circus. Some had thought that the fox had a foul smell, that it was soiling the grounds, even that it was sinful to keep an animal like this in a monastery. Flush with anger, Ioakim would persist in taking care of the little fox as long as the Abbot did not object. He shared his own food, his own bread with the animal. He let it drink from the fountain. Water belonged to no one. Its chain was long enough to allow the animal to come up to the trough to lap at the water's edge. Although the fox always finished what Ioakim served him, he began to notice that the animal's bowl was never empty. Which meant there were others who tended to the little fox. He therefore turned a deaf ear to the complaining monks. In time, they, too, came to recognize that they had to accept the existence of the little fox, give in to irresistible neighborliness. One day, right after lunch when most of the monks were walking around the courtyard, Andreas had walked straight over to the little fox, had begun playing with it. It was as though the entire monastery had been waiting for such a gesture. From then on, few monks could resist joking around with the animal, if not playing chase or hide-and-seek, at least letting it nibble at their hand, or teasing it by pretending to steal food from its bowl. The fox had become most everyone's pet, a property of the monastery. Everyone loved it.

Ioakim now thinks that the kit fox had taught the monks that even an animal deserved love. That the world contained other things worthy of love. . . . That beyond loving God, they could also love God's creatures . . . But did they acknowledge this fact? Those for whom loving an animal, caring for it, was a sin, did they not accept that human beings, animals, plants, rocks were all God's creation? Did the act of loving God require not loving His creatures?

He should have thought of these questions then, spoken out then, not now. To think these thoughts now amounts to regressing. By now, he ought to have gone beyond these ideas.

Why does one like watermelons, figs, grapes, wine? Why does one reel with the excitement of seeing them anew at the end of each summer, at the start of each winter?

They loved the animal. No one saw or noticed the chain around its neck. Even the kit fox seemed to have forgotten. If it acted annoyed by its bondage, complained about its chain, at the first hint of discontent, everyone would have rushed to unchain it. Instead, the chained animal behaved as if it lived in its own forest

Or did it seem so to him?

One November morning following a night of endless rain, Ioakim had found the kit fox violently shaking under its rags. Ioakim is shivering.

He's shivering now. There is a light breeze, a gentle wind. Not much to make one feel cold, but Ioakim is shivering. Is he still walking? Has he stopped? How can he be sure at this moment?

So much thinking, so much remembering, stopping instead of walking, almost tracing his steps back, does it all mean he doesn't want to reach that point, get to the top of the hill?

It was raining, a dense, steady rain that brought the cold along with it. The first cold of winter. The little animal was drenched, shaking violently under its rags. He had found a thick piece of woolen cloth, folded it into a bag; tearing at the corner of his mattress, he'd removed some of the padding, stuffed the bag with it; then, setting the bag in a place the rain couldn't reach, he had laid the little fox inside it with his own hands. After a while, the animal had stopped shaking, it lay brokenhearted inside its new bag. It must have fallen ill.

In the rain that came down on the courtyard along with the first cold of winter, his own robe, too, had felt much too thin that morning; he had gotten soaked right away. At first, he'd worried little about the rain; while the other monks were walking among the columns, underneath the arches, he had stepped outside, circled a few times the dry well at the center of the courtyard. Later he had joined the other monks but, unable to stay too long, he'd walked back to the mouth of the well. He had shivered, but not the way he's shivering now.

To experience this shivering now, he would have had to live through so many years — so many endless, relentless years — to live without shame, that is, to live shamelessly for having felt shame without being able to do anything about it.

He sees in this shivering the shadows that consume the reed beds, the swamp. He sees the dead swamp, the dead reed beds dying with the passing day, their defeat by time. Darkness begins thus, by consuming the dead — those who resist it the most because they know that darkness feeds on the dead.

Why has it not consumed me yet? asks Ioakim. Am I supposed to start believing that I am not dead enough yet?

The field before him prepares itself to defy death just as it has defied it every evening for years, for centuries. To defy death every evening, then to be defeated for just a few hours: If this is not a sign of being alive, of having remained undead, if this is not the essence of life, what is it? The field before him, more alive than it has been all day, is now enveloped in a fiery glow. Ioakim again closes his eyes. He can't feel his legs, they have no weight anymore. How tired he is! Yet, he still must climb to the top of the hill, discover something else while looking out, finish another sentence, experience the vain satisfaction that lends a sense of equilibrium to one's being, soul, emotions, by helping one feel justified in finishing another day just for having finished a few sentences. Then he must begin descending, never to climb again. Never to climb again

This, too, is a new notion. When did he decide never to climb again? Have I become altogether senile? he asks. He senses the tightening of a grin at the corner of his mouth. How long since — perhaps a moment, perhaps a year or a decade, he does not know, he cannot remember, but as if it has been a long time, a very long time since — he had a similar sensation, how long since he laughed to himself like this?

Is this the right time to lose his train of thought, fall into daydreaming?

He was shivering but could not stop circling around the well. Every so often, he would lift his head to look at the monks walking under the arches, but then turn his gaze back to the rain-soaked weeds, the soil — the dead, useless weeds that did nothing but emit their odor of death, while the soil, swollen with an insatiable appetite, screamed for more deaths, more weeds dying, more dead weeds. Every so often, he would catch a monk looking at him, but they would quickly look away. He knew that the monks found his behavior strange, that they wondered what sort of sin he was trying to expiate by walking in the cold rain. . . . Perhaps he was free of sins or perhaps supposed to be crushed under the weight of too many sins; either way, the idea of expiation had not even crossed his mind. Something else was in his mind — not a passing thought but a tangled knot, altogether different. Whether any of his sins or any measure of his sinfulness was part of this tangled knot, or if the tangled knot itself was among his sins, he didn't know, but what tangled his thoughts into a knot was his keen awareness that Andronikos — if he were still alive, hiding on some mountain he knew not where — would be walking under the same rain. He was walking, he was feeling cold. He had not even tried to look for him. He knew he wouldn't have been able to find him. Besides, the monastery elders must have sent search parties after him. When he realized in the cold gloom of that cold morning that he had consoled himself with these excuses for the past two months, he understood that nothing he could do — neither walking under the rain nor even shedding his robe, shirt, undergarments to walk stark naked under the rain — would suffice. He would not have been able to find him. Could he not have

Walked the streets? Asked around?

That he would not have encountered someone who had seen him, no witnesses, someone who knew him, recognized, remembered him? Could that have been possible?

Walking the streets he walked, tracing his steps, still not finding him, could this have been entirely

Since the monastery's elders had been unsuccessful in their search

The rain was harsh; his robe felt heavier though thinner at the same time; he slowed down, taking deliberate steps, circling the well like a mill horse

As those mill horses circled around the screeching of the wheel shaft, the deafening groan of the worn-out wooden socket, as their circling seemed as if it would never end

Was it important to have heard the bell when the gate was opened; should those who had been in the courtyard, should someone among them, should he, have noticed when the attendant monk had unbolted the gate with a grave, tired motion? Why did man attempt to invest ordinary events with significance after the fact, when their sole function at the time was to serve as links in a chain?

This is what he knew at the time: It had been as though the ground below the arched portal had cracked open so suddenly that no one had noticed or even sensed the arrival of Andronikos, but there he was, standing before them, in deep, stony silence.

Ioakim stands

where he stood the evening before, every evening before that, for many years. In the exact spot where he always closes his eyes for a moment, anticipating that — even though he knows every detail of the scenery by heart — he will open them to something entirely new. The woods extend behind him. He knows. In front of him, at the bottom of the steep precipice, the field once trodden by racing horses is now overtaken by a malodorous lake that serves as a breeding ground to swarms of mosquitoes. Further out, at the foot of the next hill

in the place of Palatinus, a sea almost the color of lapis-lazuli

This image is particularly stubborn. Yes, it is blue, but his eyes, his being, want a different shade of blue, one commonly used by painters; something inside him is shouting, screaming for this other blue. The three arms of the sea in the arms of the three-armed city

Eyes closed again, he is thinking of the blue. With all

his mental energy, only the blue. When the waters begin to flow, when the remote villages to the right along with the nearby villages to the left are caught in the eerie glow of the setting sun, when they begin to gasp for air, when he feels as though his head is spinning.

In place of the sea, Palatinus, with its immense, yawning mouths, the remains of the ancient palace.

How stubborn he has been in calling them mouths for years — these apertures in the walls that look nothing like mouths

When errors become habitual, habits errors, does living get at all easier when you fully accept the habit of errors

Neither the mouths nor the walls really matter. The remoteness of the sea, the three-armed sea, doesn't matter either.

What matters is this light: the suspenseful interval before day turns to night, the still-unsettled today becomes the unalterable yesterday, life becomes death, this light held in perfect balance, teetering — the more he thinks about these, the more he will lose his balance, slide toward the night, toward yesterday, toward death. . . . This light is significant.

Whether the gate was then closed or left open, whether or not the bolts were refastened, whether the monks under the arches had stood still or come out into the yard to resume their walk — eyeing each other, staring at the ground or at the arches — Ioakim can remember none of these details.

Instead he sees — recalls — himself standing alone at the well, in the middle of the garden, the courtyard, the city, the sea, the world, while Andronikos approaches him — moving less like a person walking than like a sailboat gliding toward him.

Afterwards, order had returned to the world.

The evening shadow now blankets the swamp, the

sprawling, vacant graveyard of giant horses. The land beyond the swamp turns perfectly luminescent, brilliant.

Watching the shadow play on the swamp surface, Ioakim's eyes visualize it as a phosphorescent sea. By now, this illusion only belongs to his eyes, to his heart. His skin, his shoulders have been frozen by an icy numbness, can no longer feel even the chill of the breeze.

Children's voices are silenced at meal time. Women no longer call for them. Men, too, must have fallen silent with fatigue. The church bells are stilled, as if never to ring again in this first hour of evening. In the distance, the litany of mosquitoes accentuates the silence. Those yawning mouths, the remains of imperial palaces, gather in whatever is left of the day's light to reflect it back. Even the sky cannot withstand the terracotta shades of dusk.

Just like every evening.

Ioakim thinks it's time to begin descending.

He thinks so every evening around the same time.

But this evening, it seems as though he wants to see something else. He will not descend before he sees it. As if he had made up his mind even before setting out for his walk, he now stands waiting with the patience of a man who knows what he wants.

Though neither was his mind made up nor does he know what he is waiting to see. He cannot even sense it

Or he knows it, he senses it. There are so many sentences to finish, he says to himself. There is the realization, he says, that all these ascents, all these descents should finally arrive at an end point, the end of a sentence.

But he doesn't believe it. While believing, while believing he believes, while no longer believing he believes, no longer disbelieving he disbelieves, no longer believing he disbelieves he disbelieves

What is the use of all this effort?

Is it to save his pride (as a human being who chose

to walk a different path), his human pride from the sewer with its giant mouth near the poplar under which he always sits, the mouth that, for centuries, has discharged the city's groundwater into the river, keeping the thought of the sewer forever alive in people's minds?

Is it to save his pride from this underground current that reveals its existence only at the point where it emerges into the sunlight, carrying into the mountain stream the excrement — from public squares, streets, houses, from an entire city — the torrent of excrement that washes life away?

He had not approached Andronikos, instead waited in the rain, cold

That day, what could he have said to Andronikos? What did he talk about? All this was now buried under the solid walls of the intervening years.

He has not forgotten. There is nothing to remember, except for a particular darkness that has long preoccupied his mind. When he recalls that day, he is surrounded by the same darkness: It's after the evening mass, following the cadence of certain grandiose, hallowed, reverberant, meaningless words across the dim light of the candle flames; Andronikos is standing alone at the center, his gaze fixed on the smooth curtain

that for the past few months has covered the niches that contained the icons

his steady voice declaring, "I have come to renounce the oath"

Later it would become clear that these words were not spoken by mistake, that they had not been uttered inadvertently by a man who, having spoken to no one for the past few months, was actually trying to say something else.

Perhaps here is where all sentences end, must end. When the evening's shadow begins to gnaw at, to eat away, the view ahead, from roots to leaves, from top to bottom, when the pistachios shed their outer skins that float on the surface of the darkly swelling water, here is no place to stay.

All of the sentences, all of the days, the years, the walks, the seas, beliefs, deaths, escapes, perhaps all of these end, must end, here.

Hereafter, words, inexhaustible, to the point of exhaustion

To speak from now on would be

inexhaustible words uttered to the point of exhaustion

So it was. So it had been.

By coiling around his neck an inexhaustible rope he had woven out of words, Andronikos had exhausted himself.

He sneezes. As if he's forgotten why he set out on this tiring walk, as if he was not here this evening to see what he has seen every evening over the years, Ioakim turns around, straightens his body to take deep breaths, begins to descend — rather, the descent — feeling the solid pain of his tired steps.

Darkness has long gathered over where he senses the river must be; the wind against his face is no longer soft; the setting sun is but a trace in the sky; from now on, Ioakim's eyes will be fixed on the ground. He will only watch the path, his weakening eyes have to mind the path, nothing else.

He had not considered before the possibility of speaking to the point of exhaustion; had anyone mentioned the possibility, he would not have believed it, until that day.

At first, everything seemed like a joke. An elaborate joke ill becoming the abbot, out of place in the grave solemnity of a monastery.

Was it possible that the other monks had perceived it as an actual punishment rather than a joke?

He doesn't think so. They would realize later. Then again, perhaps he would be the last to see the light. The very last.

Did Andronikos himself understand at the time the punishment given to him?

All these old questions, are they not like certain key themes in a book being summarized, enumerated, on the last pages so that they're not wasted or forgotten, though they'd been stated in the preceding hundreds of pages? He couldn't answer these questions at the time; it's unlikely that he will now.

Is it not all the more in vain to struggle, strain, resist like a child, like a foolhardy youth, an inexperienced person with immature judgment who stands on the brink of emptiness but doesn't recognize it?

It was so overcast on that morning that it had seemed as though the sun hadn't risen. But could such a thing even be possible? To say, "as though the sun hadn't risen" on the morning when Andronikos' death would begin, would it be anything more than a tired symbolism as trampled as mud? Then again, even though he had waited for the sun to rise, he saw that it didn't, more precisely, he did not see the sun rise. He knew. The sky had grown slightly brighter, nothing more. By the time one could surmise, sense, that the new day had arrived

the punishment was already being administered. There is no use in asking why. Those charged with administering the punishment had relied on man-made hours rather than the sun to determine the start of the day.

He had arrived at what at the time seemed to him like an intelligent insight: Human beings dispensed judgment, even in the name of God, according to their own scales. In retrospect, this insight no longer strikes Ioakim as particularly intelligent. Is this not something that human beings must have always recognized?

When the sky had grown bright enough that he could distinguish — perhaps also aided by habit — the earth-colored wall outside his cell's window from the dirt path that ran alongside the wall, he had descended the steps to the chamber below the church.

He was still the youngest of the monks in the monastery. No one younger had joined the order yet. When the Abbot had called on the youngest, the greenest, monk to stand watch over the defiant sinner while he endured his punishment, had he intended to destroy Andronikos' pride? Or was he trying to teach the youngest monk a lesson? Or, because at some point there had been the vague hint of a certain friendship between the two, was the Abbot trying to dole out each man his due punishment?

It's strange but, of all the questions that no longer matter, this particular question still matters. Ioakim still wonders about it; he grows neither tired nor reproachful for doing so. His mind seems to favor the last option.

Punishment, when shared, is twice as heavy. He clearly knows that now.

At first, he had watched Andronikos bent double on a straw mat, sleeping. When the Abbott entered the cell, Ioakim had stepped back, leaned against a column.

The Abbott had woken Andronikos, looked into his eyes. Why Andronikos had shown no surprise, why he'd gotten onto his feet so effortlessly — as if he had been awake for a while, perfectly alert — why he had stood upright, shaken his head, uttered, "No," with a firm voice, his lips barely moving, Ioakim would understand the reasons later, much later.

In response to this "No," the Abbott had turned back, called on Ioakim, ordering him to take Andronikos to the Monastery of Mary of the Merciful Judgment in one hour.

Eventually, Ioakim had come to understand this: His youth, his inexperience had made him the most trustworthy person to carry out the order. The Abbott had laid on his shoulders a burden he would not be able to shake off for the rest of his life.

When did he free himself from this torment?

Did he ever?

Everything had appeared ready at Mary of the Merciful Judgment, everyone seemed prepared for his role. As though this particular punishment could not be administered at their own monastery, they were sent to the most prominent monastery of the See. What Ioakim could not understand was this: in actuality, this punishment

On that day, while accompanying Andronikos to the monastery, he had found in himself the strength to mull over all these questions, to speculate about sundry things. Would one call his behavior ridiculous or shameful? That he had not recognized this until now, does it add one more indignity to his share of indignities? To recall all this, even now

The human mind is a monster. This punishment

In actuality, this punishment was not of the kind that would have been administered before a crowd to serve as a warning; neither were any witnesses deemed necessary other than a neophyte monk, also considered to be the convict's friend. But why at this monastery?

Why had Andronikos gained such importance? Why was he being sent to this monastery? Until now many who refused to take the oath had endured myriad forms of torture, openly or in secret. This was common knowledge. Torture for those who refused the new order, death to those who proved intractable. Why were they paying so much attention to someone like Andronikos, a thoroughly unexceptional man, one who had not divulged his sentiments even to his fellow monks, by all accounts an unlikely rebel-rouser?

Ioakim would understand only much later that a ceremony, a sacrifice of some sort, was being performed in the name of the public.

Inside the cell, once the abbot of Mary of the Merciful Judgment also received "No" for an answer, two soldiers had stood over Andronikos. One of them had poked him with the tip of his lance, asked him to begin.

Everything had seemed no different from a staged play.

As it grew dark in the evening, Ioakim had been startled by the voice calling him, "Ioakim, wake up, I need you, still need you, bear with me a while longer." He remembers it as if today. He had dozed off. Opening his eyes, he had noticed Andronikos standing up, under the narrow window. The pale light seeping through the grillwork had quickly died out. The guard had changed, his shoulder buckle shining a bit higher than the previous one's. Ioakim could not make out his face but the shorter guard appeared to be sleeping in the corner, doubled up, a shape in which the human body most resembles an urn.

"I still need you," Andronikos was saying.

In the fifty years since, much had happened, much had changed, Ioakim had spent an entire life. Is he truly remembering or fabricating, fashioning, a past?

He does not want to be someone caught in the memories of a past long dead, walking down a darkening path without thinking anything new, returning to his home, his country, as if returning to his grave. Did he not wish that this evening were different from all the evenings past?

In needing Ioakim, Andronikos had needed the presence of someone who would listen, who would understand him. He had not yet reached the point at which he would no longer be weary of being seen as — weary of being, of knowing that he actually was — someone who talked to himself while in the company of others, he had not yet crossed the threshold beyond which he would no longer feel such weariness.

Ioakim was not allowed to speak. Not even to respond to questions. When he'd tried to do so in the morning, the guard had rebuked him. Whose order was this? Was there even such an order? He didn't know.

He had consequently been able to lend an ear to Andronikos while at the same time thinking sundry thoughts — either things he remembered or thoughts prompted by what he heard. Even though his mind had functioned on a separate plane from his ears, the two faculties had seemed to complement one another, neither one entirely drawing him away from the other.

He tries to remember the morning when Andronikos had returned to the monastery. He couldn't remember it when he was at Mary of the Merciful Judgment; he can't remember it now either. Andronikos had come to stand in front of him, but after that there was — there still is, a void; what happened after is impossible to recall. Andronikos had told him, "You seem to have grown up." His voice was strange, muffled — he remembers this detail well — whereas at Mary of the Merciful Judgment, it sounded most resonant, full, clear. Of course, early on, that is, on the first day.

Then he had extended his hand, laid it on Ioakim's shoulder, gently pulled at the tresses running down his nape. Afterwards, he'd gone into the Abbott's cell. Ioakim's mental void begins here, lasts until "I came to renounce the oath," during the evening mass.

There is another void.

During which the monks must have eaten their meals, said their prayers, then retired to their beds. A void that lasts from the time when Andronikos was taken to the cell in which he would spend the night, to the time when Ioakim could distinguish — perhaps also aided by habit — the earth-colored wall outside his cell's window from the dirt path that ran alongside the wall. These are voids he could not fill either with his life, which he did not live, or with Andronikos' life, which he did not get to share.

He is certain of one thing about the void: He did not talk, rather, he was reluctant to talk, to Andronikos about the kit fox. Perhaps because he was weary or felt ashamed, or because he did not even think about the little animal. He can't even remember whether the fox visited him or not.

On that first day at Mary of the Merciful Judgment, Andronikos had filled these voids with his share of details, but Ioakim could not find himself in Andronikos' narrative, could not determine his place inside these voids.

Does it even matter? Not anymore, but did it matter then?

Ioakim was wrong to think that he had shared the punishment. He had in no way shared it. He had merely been carried away with the assumption that the impressions of the punishment amounted to experience. Perhaps he had, for about a day or so, provided support to Andronikos. But after that day or so, the man had no need for support.

At one point he had described the island to which he 'd escaped, the walls he had built by himself, an edifice he had built encircling the spring. To his mind, it was a house, a shelter, as much as it was a sanctuary.

Then one morning, he had suddenly come to realize the futility of his efforts.

Perhaps he could have built sturdier walls, separated the sanctuary from the shelter, worked year after year to adorn it. Others in the past had built such structures. Even if there had been no one before him, he could have been the first of the builders. He could have asked the fishermen — he had avoided them at first, later approached them reluctantly, fearfully — to bring him the materials, the provisions he would have needed, he could have formed friendships with them, planted gardens, tended to animals.

The futility of these ideas had occurred to him as if at a moment of acute clarity. Everything he made would have been but an addition, an appendage. He would not have moved forward — not even by a single step. He'd realized that he had arrived at a wall; his forehead, his nose, his knees, his fingernails were pressed against it. If one could not go beyond the wall, what did it matter if one spent an entire life adorning it?

To go beyond the wall, he had to come back. Only by coming back — no, coming back would not have sufficed — by continuing to reject whatever he had escaped from, more than that, by explaining his resolve openly, in a manner that everyone could recognize without even the slightest trace of uncertainty, by accepting in the end what he had done, by submitting to all its consequences, only then would he be able to move forward. Only then, the step he had taken would gain meaning, his deeds would escape evanescence.

While Andronikos spoke, the child facing him had accepted his every word; he had asked no questions, no questions worth asking had come to his mind. Even if he had a question, how could he ask it, given that he was forbidden to speak? Little by little, Andronikos had given up staring into his eyes, in the waning hours, he had altogether stopped looking at his face while speaking. Near the evening of the second day, Ioakim had realized with dread that Andronikos was no longer speaking to him. Or to the guards, the walls, or the ceiling. He was not even speaking into the void. By the evening of the third day, what he was doing could not even be considered speaking to himself.

Or could it be that Ioakim was starting to grow

drowsy, his mind dizzy with swarming thoughts? Not just his mind, his senses, his flesh, but his entire being growing numb?

Still, if Ioakim had shared at all in Andronikos' punishment, it would have been in the following days. The one being punished was eating, drinking, walking about, sitting or standing. Ioakim, too, was eating the same food, sitting or standing. Every so often, he was dozing off — that was the only difference. More precisely, he was allowed to doze off. When he dozed off — with each passing day, the time he spent sleeping would increase, each nap lasting a shorter amount of time, but at closer intervals — Ioakim could not be sure whether or not Andronikos continued speaking, but the guards — who took turns sleeping — must have forced him to keep speaking by prodding or kicking him, as this was their only duty. At times, the guards, too, felt tired. While the one was asleep, the other, who was supposed to keep listening, would drop his head down to doze off from time to time. In those periods when Ioakim, too, had dozed off, he could not be sure that anyone was awake. Except for Andronikos — only he was not allowed to fall asleep. This was what felt like Ioakim's own torture. To be able to fall asleep, to remain silent, in front of the man who was slowly being killed by a form of torture that had started like a play at first but quickly lost any resemblance to a play, more precisely, a form of torture that was quickly becoming only too real. Ioakim's share was the opposite face of the punishment: to sleep before the one who was kept awake, to remain silent before the one who was forced to speak.

Ioakim still can't decide, which was the torture? What had finished off Andronikos? Sleeplessness or being forced to speak? Or the exhaustion from both?

When he urinated for the first time, he had stopped talking, until the guards prodded him to continue. Afterwards, he had learned to raise his voice when he urinated. Two or three times, he was taken to a hole outside. Then, too, he was forced to keep talking. Ioakim knew this, because he could still hear his voice.

He is at the foot of the hill again. The sky has grown considerably dark. The bells must have tolled a long while ago, but he is not aware. His teeth chatter from the cold, his jawbones rattle. Still, he kneels down under the lush, solitary pistachio tree the shape of which he has managed to make out, sense, even in the dark. Far ahead, countless points of light, the windows of the cells in which his friends — his children, his sheep — are in their beds. They must have begun worrying about his absence. Anxious like a flock of sheep missing their shepherd. But he wants to stay outside a little longer. He wants to feel the cold, to tremble, beyond any hope for warmth. There are still unfinished matters. He cannot go inside.

En route to Ravenna
as if on a trip, an excursion
he was running away as everyone knew
on the ship that was carrying away a family, servants, slave
wealth, provisions, oils, fabrics, gold that belonged to noble Michael who grudgingly had to leave his mansion behind

Ioakim had heard that the noble's slave was from the Orient, but had not thought of asking him what part of the ocean known as the Orient he was from. He can't even recall his name, except that it was an odd name, like all Oriental names

One night, he'd told Ioakim a fairy tale; it was a night when the sea was somehow perfectly calm, a night of oppressive heat when a cool dampness clung to one's skin.

It must have been an Oriental tale. It's strange that he can still remember it.

Perhaps it's not strange.

Some details elude him: where the architect was from, who he was, why he had agreed to undertake the task.

He does remember this: An architect is instructed to build a palace with hundreds of, thousands of, cut stones of various colors. A palace such that whoever enters it should feel perfectly at home, know which room is where, which stairway leads where, which door opens to which room; but at the same time, the palace has to be so extraordinary, built so ingeniously, that whoever enters it should know, recognize right away that he neither has seen nor will ever get to see another place like it in his lifetime.

The architect is given one more instruction. No two stones of identical color can be set either side by side or one over the other, except once, in one singular instance throughout the immense palace.

So the architect gets to work, applying his cunning, his utmost mastery, supervising the completion of the first row of stones. But the difficulties he encounters during the second row prove quite daunting. So he orders the workers to tear down the first row, deciding to start over by building up one of the corners. After getting a few rows completed, he moves to building another corner. To avoid tearing down what he has built. Each time he notices that a pair of same-colored stones would have to be set side by side, he leaves that wall segment to get started on another segment. The thought that he is allowed only one exception disheartens him so much that he keeps postponing the exception, thinking he might need it later. Days, months, years pass like this; he grows old, one foot is already in the grave, as they say, each morning may be the start of his last day, each night may be his last; then, all of a sudden, he realizes

He realizes that, though his workers have long abandoned him — in reality, he had pushed them away — and he's been toiling alone for years in a dreadful frenzy, he has somehow managed to gather inside him all the patience his workers have lost, to recover deep in the heart of his heart all the patience he's spent on his workers, absorb their strength in his own arms in order to fill the entire plot assigned to him with wall fragments, waiting to be connected. Even if he has enough strength or life left in him to connect these walls, he has completely cleared his mind of the rules according to which the palace was supposed to have been built; the finished structure will not even resemble a barn that could shelter animals, much less a palace at once extraordinary, at once familiar to everyone. There is neither a palace nor a building in place, not even the notion of one or the other.

Only one question had crept its way into young Ioakim's mind that night: So what if he didn't build it? What if he didn't toil?

At that age, a person is predisposed to renounce a duty rather than understanding it....

The fairy tale he heard that night probably contained details that illuminated or answered this question. He doesn't recall. Still, those details couldn't have explained to a young mind such as Ioakim's why someone would agree to play a game that would cause him to squander his entire life. For Ioakim, the memory of Andronikos, his way of being, had permeated his life so completely that he'd failed to see how he resembled the architect, or, at the least, he had failed to think that such a resemblance could ever exist.

The Oriental slave

At the end of his story — it had seemed to last for hours — the Oriental slave had asked Ioakim the following question: What did you learn? What does this fairy tale want to tell you? Without waiting for Ioakim's response, he'd risen to his feet; walking away, he'd said, "Life." Nothing more.

A few nights later, the poor man was stabbed to death by one of the sailors. As if it had to have been so. That man from the Orient was meant to be the hero of a story with a definitive ending.

Fragments of memories. That man who was so dread-stricken that he died before he could set side by side even the one pair of same-colored stones

He had to have died. Ioakim cannot recall the rest of the fairy tale

The architect who died

To gather those unraveled balls of yarn, if but once before dying, to bring them together, to be able to believe that he has woven a thread

En route to Ravenna, he had been happy. Hopeful that, by escaping, he would get closer to what Andronikos had done by returning. That he would recall the Oriental slave's fairy tale tonight, under the pistachio tree — his teeth chattering, his jawbones rattling — that he would discover in this fairy tale a new meaning for himself, about the way he has lived

He strains to rise to his feet. Good that he has a staff. He resumes walking toward his bed, his tomb, his dome that is beginning to grow luminous, toward his sky.

His sky of miniature colored tiles — but of the kind that heeds no law or stricture against setting same-colored tiles side by side — spanning the interior surface of a dome that, little by little, is coming alive, beginning to show the way to eternity; the arches that support this dome

His home — its likeness, its shadow — in this alien country, his sanctuary soon to be his tomb

His country, the land where he is the sovereign

The temple's dome, its arches

He will revive the dying fire in Ravenna.

How had he made himself believe in all these notions, acting without a tinge of irony as though his life depended on this fabrication?

He can't understand.

Can he not?

He'll go a little further, pass under the outer arch, walk down the arcade; as he passes under one arch after another, he'll be approaching the point that seemingly has imbued his entire life with meaning; the young monks will gather around him, wait in reverence for him to explain his delay, to allay their anxiety that his absence was not due to anything of importance

His children, his flock of sheep. Their shepherd. . . .

Though most of them

Though most of them no longer wonder what the runaways were running from, why those refugees sought refuge in this temple, what this place means to them; never mind wondering, most of them don't even know enough to wonder. The young ones were born fifteen, twenty, twenty-five years ago. In other words, they're the children born ten, fifteen years after Ioakim arrived here.

And does life ever cease? People seem to forget this easily. That life doesn't cease, that it changes, that it will go on changing. That the children, when they grow up, will know a different world, that they will live in a world altogether different from the one their fathers had known

Silently Ioakim laughs to himself, laughs at himself. Is it not laughable that, just a little while ago, when he started climbing the hill, he was determined not to descend unless he made a new discovery, then, even when descending, he leaned against a tree, waiting, delaying his return as much as he did? Is it not laughable that a person, even at his age, cannot estimate his own strength, his abilities, grasp the meaning of time?

What he sought was solitude. Since he couldn't prolong this solitude outside, would it not be best to do so inside his cell? He recalled the septuagenarian monk's seven-day penitential fast, though not when he was on the hill or along the path, rather tonight, when he returned to the monastery

It is now perfectly obvious.

He now understands the monk's penitential fast. What he had done in those seven solitary days was not penitence. It was what Ioakim now wants to do, what he realizes he will do, what he decides to do. The ancient monk had reconciled his accounts before pulling down the shutters for good. He must have succeeded, since he had died on the eighth day.

He laughs. Once upon a time

Many times, in various situations, various places, he did consider taking his own life. He laughs at the thought.

That he considered it, that he decided against it, that he could decide against it, that he never ceased deciding against it . . . he laughs.

Mostly it was the fear of God that made him decide against it, although a few times, it was the fear of death. At times he thought suicide would be cowardly, a false form of heroism. He also thought that death would be absurd, that it would solve nothing.

He laughs now.

That septuagenarian monk, what kind of a life did he lead? Ioakim doesn't know, but being found dead following the seven-day penitence — seven, eight, ten, three . . . how absurd to venerate a mere number — would it be a fitting end for Ioakim? Would God want it? He no longer cares to know.

He laughs that he hasn't been able to consider any of this until now.

Would he die at the end of his penitence? He doesn't know. He can't.

Neither will he try to die; he doesn't care to hasten his death.

He laughs. To hasten death. A laughable proposition.

In the morning he'll retreat. Start his penitence. Reconcile his accounts.

Could he have imagined, starting out on his evening walk, that he would attain such calm, such peace of mind? But now he knows one more thing. What he truly needed, what he has been searching for. It is this calm, this peace of mind, this shadow of attainment. Now all the sentences can end. Compared to the ancient monk, Ioakim lacks one thing: the experience of having lived twenty years in stony silence. The deaf monk's reconciliation had to have actually lasted for twenty years plus seven days.

For that matter, Ioakim has been climbing the hill for years, has he not? These walks could be added to the accounting.

Now his laughter carries a tinge of surprise. These childish negotiations, if they are supposed to mark the beginning of penitence, of reconciliation — why not, why should he not call it so — does he not seem to lack the seriousness the task deserves? Is he being too cavalier?

But he mustn't stop now. No matter what, even if he makes mistakes, becomes laughable in his own eyes, even if he denigrates himself, he must prevail. He's been chewing the cud for fifty years; he must now swallow.

This evening, he said whatever he needed to say to his monks, his disciples, he offered them whatever he needed to offer. He allayed their curiosity, reminded them not to neglect their prayers. He did, he said, what is expected of a father, of a guide. He glanced at the colorful tiles along the edge of the scaffolding that stood under the dome, the tiles that began to hint at the magnificent artwork being patiently uncovered. The day would come when this interior dome would be fully uncovered, its magnificence fully restored, revealing the essence of God's wisdom to everyone. Then it will be said, this temple

This temple, it will be said, is a monument erected by those people determined to oppose every form of schism, every person or nation that rebels against God.

Then much more will be spoken, many more overworked expressions will be repeated.

Everyone will forget the reason why the Grand Bishop in Rome, the enemy of Byzantium, of the Byzantine church, had taken the very same church under his wing, why he had offered its adherents this temple as a safe haven. No one will recall that he had been in rivalry with the Emperor who had held religion captive to his will.

Is Ioakim the only wise person? There's no time for

such nonsense. If the pope is protecting the Byzantine church against the Byzantine Emperor, if he is granting the church the opportunity to survive on his soil, the right to build its own sanctuary, he is doing so because he knows, he believes, that he will sooner or later strangle it on his own soil, force it into his own world.

He was, we should say, he knew. He had to be aware. How could he not be? His spies, who knows ever since when

All of them, in the end, even if Ioakim were dead

Those who live, those who survive, all of them will at first live among the refugees in exile, then begin to mix into the ocean they have entered, eager to melt in its waters.

But it's too late to think about these matters. Ioakim, leader of the refugees, has done all he was supposed to do. Strange, is it not, that a man who believes he has done everything he could in order to save the thing he struggled to save, realizes at the end of his life that his own hands have been chiefly responsible for strangling it.

For the septuagenarian monk, espousing a life of stillness to escape the molds — whether or not he succeeded — had meant he could neither destroy nor save anything. Ioakim had broken this chain from the very start. To save, to be free

He had strangled it.

The kit fox.

At the mention of the act . . .

Today he can neither free himself nor escape from the animal.

The little fox, the lock that will hang on his book of life.

A trite cliché befitting self-important braggarts.

One of the keys

A lock with many keys?

My God, Ioakim thinks, can man never escape being laughable?

The link. He has been looking for this link. He recognizes it now.

The kit fox had been ill. Although its shivering had abated, it had been lying listlessly in its pile of rags. But by the time he had remembered the animal again — the night when he flung his exhausted body out of bed to rush out into the dark courtyard — nine days had passed. Andronikos had died little by little in the course of these nine days. Proving time after time the colossal futility of heroism, its boundless absurdity, he had died, becoming in the process a hero himself. But Ioakim was alive; aside from his exhaustion, his self-reproach mixed with disgust, he had no troubles while he stood beside the fox.

He had pushed his hand through the folds of rags, looking for the animal's mouth, waiting for the sharp little teeth to sink into his flesh. Instead his hand had come to rest, quite unexpectedly, on a parched muzzle burning like fire. The mouth wouldn't open, the teeth wouldn't sink into his flesh. The animal was still sick. The food had been crusting in its bowl, untouched. He'd noted this by feeling the food with his other hand. Perhaps the fox would die.

From hunger, from thirst. Dying from hunger was probably more agonizing than dying from illness.

He wonders whether he had really meant what he had thought at the time.

Tormented by Andronikos' death, had he decided that another being he so loved had to die, too?

Loving himself, he had to kill himself, too. . . .

First the fox, then himself.

Pulling the animal out of its bedding, he had pressed its limp body against his chest, unfastened its chain. It had trembled in his arms. Perhaps from fear or the scorching fever.

He had walked to the gray, coffin-like stone tub

plunged the fox in the water, his swiftness or his rage entirely uncharacteristic of him.

Even now, as he recalls the events, he's seized by torment, as if someone is cutting into his flesh, tearing it open. Even now.

All the thoughts, rather, all the associations during that never-ending

During that never-ending — his arm thrust almost to the elbow in the frigid water that had soaked up the iciness of the stone, of the sky, the contractions in his arm, one after another, set off each time his fingers tightened, his wrist hardened like stone, each time the little fox struggled to escape — all the associations during that never-ending stretch of time

Whether these had been his actual thoughts or associations at the time that he was now casting in words, he can't tell, though the difference no longer seems to matter.

He was aware of one thing. He was drowning the little fox. The one he had loved madly, cared for, raised, protected from others, kept alive in spite of others, maybe even succeeded in making others love as well. He thought he knew why he was drowning it. He considered many reasons. Which, therefore, meant that he didn't know why he was drowning it. He wanted to save the animal from disease, from dying of hunger. True, he would learn much later that the sick could be killed in order to spare them the suffering. What he meant by saving the animal from hunger was saving it from the state of starvation, the inability to eat

— a consideration that brought him closer to Andronikos. When Ioakim could tell that the animal was hungry — by the way it pattered about, now gruffly now impishly — Ioakim would set out the food, then eagerly wait: Would it like the food or not? Eat it or not? When the fox began eating, the happiness Ioakim experienced had several layers: By choosing to eat, the fox was accepting what he offered; it wasn't afraid, didn't hesitate to eat in front of him; though chained, the animal didn't miss its native woods, or the food it would have found there; in fact, it trusted him, it was able to love the hand that brought its food; it accepted his friendship ... Ioakim would watch silently. As he would later silently watch Andronikos stuff his mouth with morsel after morsel of food, chewing, swallowing — perhaps even before completely swallowing it — stuffing another in, so that his mouth never remained empty, even for a moment, so that he could not be forced to speak, until the very end of the meal. The sadness Ioakim felt at the time was itself far from simple. Three days later Andronikos had uttered the words that formed a bridge, probably for the last time, to the reality outside his mind. "Food," Andronikos had said, "eating food — as much as — it revives me — as much as — it lends me strength — it keeps me — further away — from death — yet this torture — since it does not — does not appear — it will end — soon — since — they are — waiting — for me to — die — or go mad — since — they seem — determined — not to let — me live — it would be — sensible — if — I accepted — death — We — decided — to play — the game — but — no reason — to prolong — it — do you — not think so — Ioakim"

In the deluge of words that had lasted for three days, Ioakim must not have recognized right away that these words had carried particular significance, or that they were being spoken to him. Once he recognized, he had considered two possible responses, in the end settling on a third.

Instead of nodding "yes" or "no," as he should have, he had closed his eyes, shut them tightly, stuck his fists against his ears. Then, looking at Andronikos once again, he had found his face emptied of expression, except for a vague, faraway smile. After that, Andronikos had only sipped water, probably to keep speaking.

Andronikos had died from either sleeplessness or talking endlessly, or the exhaustion from the combination of the two, but not from hunger. Hunger must have tired him out at the most.

It's not so easy to die from hunger. The peasants living around the swamp can ingest little else than herbs or seeds when they get sick, but they don't die very easily. Hunger, by itself, would have prolonged Andronikos' misery for days. Hunger alone

This reasoning, too, has two sides.

If he believes that Andronikos had not died from hunger, Ioakim's anguish (of having shut his eyes, stuck his ears) will lessen; but if he doesn't believe it, then his mind can convince itself of the need to drown the kit fox.

Both of these are false. True fallacies. False truths.

One thing had not killed Andronikos: shame.... That much is certain. Sleeplessness, talking endlessly, would exhaust a person, gradually killing him. Refusing food (they had not forced him to eat, whether out of goodness or evil; besides, the goodness or evil of torturers, of servants of the law who are duty bound to administer the torture, is unthinkable, should not even be a consideration; they are absolute beings, entirely beyond good or evil) would bring death closer, expedite it. Yet, had Andronikos believed that he would not die, must not die, or at the least, did not have to die, he might have been able to withstand the ordeal. Instead, he had seemed to accept death from the outset. Not just Andronikos but Ioakim, too. A corpse had to be carried out of this cell.

One corpse.

Nine days later.

The corpse of the one who had lain on the ground for two days, thrashing about every so often like a drunk, someone who had been actually drunk, not drunk with anything he had consumed but drunk with speaking, drunk with letting go, drunk with air, the one whose words, caught in the rush of an unintelligible garble, had sounded as if arriving from faraway places.

Only then, at the very end, Ioakim had been able to lift his head — his senses overwhelmed by the crisp air, the black frost — dragging his feet toward his monastery

None of this is about remembering this or that; in reality, he's not even thinking about the one who died. He is merely sorting out his accounts now.

Perhaps, too, trying to postpone the kit fox's death a little longer.

Maybe the little animal had not reconciled to death. Ioakim had decided that it had to die.

That was all.

No one would have tortured the fox; no one had sentenced it to torture. Following an animal's death, one could say, at the most, "It had been sick, was not eating; not much we could do. . . ."

But deciding that it should die by drowning rather than from hunger didn't mean compassion. It meant murder. It meant taking a God-given life. Without seeking permission that no one could grant, by assuming a measure of authority that nothing could justify, by exercising this authority as if it were his right. . . . The man who did this had been an accomplice in the murder of a human being, but now he would be the outright murderer of the animal. He who acted in this manner, knowingly, willfully, would have forfeited the right to a life of any significance or the ability to respect himself, even if others respected him.

After years of thinking, Ioakim still can't decide. In the course of human life or the life of societies, is there no circumstance, even one, just one, that renders the act of killing beneficial, if not beneficial, at least necessary, therefore justified? He doesn't think so, he isn't persuaded in the least.

As he kept talking, Andronikos had uttered the words fear, cowardice, betrayal, dishonor. Whether coherent or delirious, not once had he confessed to a malicious thought or deed on his part. It was perhaps this purity that had made Andronikos a hero — even if no one knew. As for Ioakim, while no one would find out (he would take every measure necessary so no one would find out) that he had drowned the little fox, destroyed a weak, defenseless life, Ioakim would never become a hero. He would never become one because he wanted to become one. In the face of Andronikos' deeds, his torture, his death, Ioakim had experienced a form of exhilaration that urged him toward heroism, that would keep urging him. But if he carried this guilt, if he could carry this guilt inside him

Perhaps this, above all else, was the truth.

Indeed, once he acknowledged his guilt, his imperfection — the crack, the void in his being — never again would he get carried away with himself or anybody else.

Nor would he let himself or anyone else be a hero.

He came to expect nothing from anyone. Now he knows that he will be scorned, not for the evil he committed, but for what was at most an error committed with a heart full of benevolent intent.

A time may come when the scorn is forgotten, can be forgiven, when it no longer seems relevant. That is as far as he can think. Then he'll be left with one thing — in all its beauty, in all its horror. The one thing that no one has known, that has made him who he is. . . .

Had it taken very long for the fox to die? He still remembers how, long after the animal had stopped struggling, he had pulled his arm out of the water as if pulling out a tree branch, how the limp, dreadfully exhausted body of the fox had dangled between his icy, stony fingers, how, afterwards, he had scanned the courtyard, expecting to find it illuminated by the dawn.

Then, with his lifeless hand — the hand that would never again attempt anything heroic — he had tied the chain around the lifeless neck of the kit fox, then cast the animal back in the water.

The next morning, while he listened to the monks' sorrowful account — *the fox must have felt thirsty at night, weakened with fever, it must have fallen into the stone trough, the chain caught around its feet must have kept it from coming up to the surface* — Ioakim's numbed mind had allowed only the faint glimmer of a thought: that, when he was tying the chain around the fox's neck, he had not thought through as far. . . .

Now, too, dawn may be near, the hour of light.

All these hours of struggle were of course not about remembering yet again how he had killed the kit fox, but at the moment he feels drained, emptied out. He might see dawn's arrival while falling asleep in this emptiness.

But dawn is not near. Neither is he sleepy.

Ravenna

There was the time before Ravenna.

Certain men had appeared in the city, secretly talking

about the valley in Cappadocia. These men were all different, different in complexion, different in their leanness, their famished bodies, different in attire. Though they had one thing in common.

The strange hunger in their eyes.

Drawing near you with their eyes fixed on the ground, the men were perhaps unremarkable at first, but once they looked up, stared into your eyes, you could not ignore where they had come from.

They spoke about the valley. That it was a sanctuary created by God. That no emperor's hand could easily touch it. That, even if armies were sent there, they would quickly abandon the hope of controlling the people who lived in the tens of thousands of hollows along the hills.

This valley, as described by those men with the strange gaze — who approached you without looking up, who kept watching the sea with you while they spoke, as if addressing the sea or the sky — had, over time, begun to assume a magic aura, glowing with a dreamy brilliance in the eyes, the hearts of many.

Every so often, when someone disappeared, the news would spread quickly. If a monk from a monastery at the other end of the city were to disappear overnight, the news would, by the next evening, have spread to every corner of the city. With each passing month, fewer people were or acted outraged at the runaway monks — *ungrateful traitors*, they would shout, *those who spurn our illustrious Emperor's benevolence deserve to die by torture.* The escapes began to carry meaning. The dissidents were coming to realize — or assume — that, in solidarity, they were gaining a new strength. Perhaps there were persons whose disappearance had nothing to do with dissent, but they, too, were counted among the escapees, in order to advance a new vocation, a new philosophy, a new virtue: Escape. It had come to be seen as an ideal, a form of resistance, a means of heroism, at the same time, a new means of oppression. . . .

Young, naïve, Ioakim was quickly drawn into this wave of escape, but for a long time managed to keep his feet anchored to the seafloor. By the time he might have been able to release his feet, to surrender his body to the sea, either the wave had lost its force or he no longer cared to be carried away.

During the early months, Ioakim could not imagine that escape might follow a different course from Andronikos' own escape to the island. Andronikos had left but he had to return. He knew why he had escaped, why he had to return. He did not resemble in the least those who escaped to the valley. They were escaping to safeguard an ideology. Andronikos had escaped to safeguard his integrity, he had returned, accepted death, for the same reason, so that no one could accuse him of selfishness. Ioakim would not be able to endure torture.

Because he would not be able to endure torture, he could not imagine returning. If he escaped, he would not return. Yet if he stayed, his life would remain untroubled. Only by escaping would he join the rebels' ranks, cut off the path of return.

For a long time, he was spurred as much by desire as by fear.

Those who did not escape would soon become objects of shame; they were already becoming so. Familiar faces were beginning to appear among the visitors from Cappadocia. Those who had stayed away long enough to be forgotten were now returning to persuade their friends to join them in the valley. Fugitives from the law, they no longer feared being caught, or rather, being turned in. They also approached Ioakim a few times.

At first, they described the valley, the authentic monastic life in the true monasteries that one found there.

They spoke of the beauty, the bounty, the vineyards widening little by little, the herds growing.

They described the cells, the houses, the churches carved into hill after hill throughout the valley. Later on some of them began to bring up the topic of his youth, trying to take advantage of it, to pressure him into leaving. Gradually, however, they must have decided that he was a hard field to plow, since he was accosted less frequently by the visitors — those men with the faraway gaze, telling stories of the valley.

One day he realized that no one encouraged him to escape anymore, no one challenged or even reproached him for refusing to escape. What he felt on that day must have been something akin to hurt, something akin to sadness. Ah, youth.

He did grow older. Old enough that he could imagine escaping, not the way Andronikos or others had, but escaping all the same. More than a few monks in the monastery were younger than him now.

He can't sleep. For hours, it seems, he's been remembering the past, as if telling himself a fairy tale. Even the moment when he thought of dawn, the hour of light, how far away even that moment feels. . . . And sleep

He isn't sure whether he's dozing off or not, but given how he has been recounting the past events without interruption

It must be the early hours of night.

He wants for sleep to come as much as he doesn't

If he can sleep, he'll release himself from the endless chain of thoughts. He'll break the chain; rather, it will break on its own.

Otherwise, he doesn't have the heart to stop, to break the chain willingly.

Not having the heart may be a sign of his fatigue. A while back — when, never mind when — he didn't want to stop. Now, he just doesn't have the heart.

He started something this evening. He will finish it; he must.

He must learn humility in the face of the smallness, the insignificance of his task.

Humility had ceased to be a virtue among the people in the valley. Now he is certain of that. They were proud of their otherness, their independence; as if they had formed a new nation, they were calling everyone to desert, to add to their numbers, trying to persuade everyone to cross to their side.

They resorted to every tactic that promised success, stopping at nothing. They were dizzy with the valley's invulnerability. The larger the community, the stronger they felt.

Was it then or sometime later?

Ioakim had started asking himself questions. He would then ask the same questions to those who came from the valley, men with hungry brilliance in their eyes. But instead of responding, they began avoiding him altogether.

Were they determined to gather in the valley every citizen who did not renounce the old faith? Would that even be possible? Even if they gathered everyone there, they wouldn't be able to, rather, they wouldn't want to, leave the valley which, being easy to defend, was their only safe haven; how could an isolationist group of believers compel the State to reaffirm the old faith?

Perhaps these were somewhat childish questions. He never got answers.

According to their accounts, on those hills along the valleys densely covered with cones — like the prickly fur on a startled cat's back — with chimneys — like the chimneys of extinguished hearths, most plugged up with rocks — the monks made up the majority of the growing population. An army of monks who, on their own, had no chance of increasing their population, who depended on the faithfulness of other new arrivals, whose number kept growing, intent on going nowhere.

Yet, the monks who left were perhaps the ones whom the decrees had constrained the least.

No one really meddled with their freedom or really persecuted them. The scribes' monasteries in particular, like Ioakim's, became sanctuaries for those who wanted to escape oppression. The monks crowding into these monasteries seemed oblivious to all the tasks that might benefit from their skill, lost themselves instead in scribing or debate, certain that one day the old belief would

Ioakim sees no point in remembering so much of the past. . . . He understands. Remembering is another form of escape. Regardless, I must keep walking, he thinks, keep moving forward on this path. His resolve makes it easier for him to acquiesce. Ease is actually nothing more than self-deception.

No, not so.

Not self-deception.

When there is a shortcut, when he can choose the shortcut, taking instead the longest road, without knowing whom or what he's against — without anticipating or understanding — anxious to save time somehow, turning right, turning left, running into dead-ends, walking back. . . .

He ought to tie the thread where it broke.

At least, he ought to try.

While sharing Andronikos' torture

He had shared Andronikos' torture — at the most — by remaining silent

If someone were to tell him now that, ever since, he has been weighed down by torture's silent face, would Ioakim deny it or call it a lie?

That he has come this far, made it to this day — out of breath, weighed down

In other words, for the shame of choosing silence, for the shame of tolerating this shame

In other words, for the shame of accepting everything as it happened

In other words, when he could have done something to dispel this shame, delving instead into the remotest corners of his mind, the farthest recesses of his heart, in order to seize, to bring out into daylight elaborate, forceful, unassailable explanations to justify his actions

For the shame of those actions that in fact get justified by such explanations

To blame himself, to look for those ingenious explanations to blame himself . . . is this not just another path that leads him to the same place?

As much as it's true that he hasn't been able to rid himself of the shame or that, whenever he attempted to speak of this shame, he squandered his life with empty chatter, it would be just as false now to attempt scrutinizing the accounts, weighing the losses against the gains, of a shop, a life, or a book nearing its end. The task ought to belong to the angels, or to those who would live after him.

The architect

Aware that he was allowed to set two same-colored stones side by side only once, that doing so would have forced him into a snare from which only death could free him, he had chosen to do nothing, absolutely nothing, trying to postpone as much as possible walking into that snare; paralyzed with fear, he still had had to face the angel of death when he came calling at the appointed hour; the surprise, the remorse, the despair

To what extent is it appropriate to assign these feelings to the architect ... he no longer cares

Rather than giving in to hopelessness, emptiness, nothingness, if only he had the courage to set those stones side by side, to accept the natural course of a life, to live

Without hesitation, without fear, fully cognizant of his act, feeling its gravity, acknowledging its worth

If he could set those two stone side by side at some point during his endeavor, his wall, if he could set those two stones side by side

Ioakim's walls come crashing down, all those walls that, over the years, multiplied his inner divisions, hardened them, they all come crashing down now with a deafmute's deafening moan.

The stones become weightless. In the face of the absurdity of such a childish notion near the end of a very long life.

Sunlight fills the spaces created by the collapsed walls; the spaces — like bellies cut open, like palaces long sealed in darkness — greet the sunlight, as if defying the sun, taunting it; the flood of light — like the three-armed sea roaring over the fields, embankments, mountains collapsing

fields, embankments, mountains collapsing with earthshaking tremors —

Illuminating the spaces heretofore unilluminated, drowning a desert in water.

If only the architect had been able to place those two stones side by side, would he not have squandered his life a little less?

Ioakim had not considered this question on the voyage to Ravenna, neither could he have. Yet, what had been guiding him at the time was nothing other than this question.

His mind racing like a child sliding down an icy slope, Ioakim is now trying to chase after his thoughts, to catch them, gather them in, hold onto them.

As if defying humility, the humility of a man who wished to surrender his being to God, as if renouncing this humility, Ioakim is thinking that

His desire to be perfect, flawless, infallible, his proud desire, sets him farther away from God; even though one must be humble before God

How else can one measure life's worth unless by spending it as a human among humans, by struggling to be good, to be perfect, by human measures; still, despite the beauty of this struggle

Failings, transgressions, too, ought to have their own beauty; even if he were to fail

In all fairness, the sole measure of one's goodness or malice depends, of necessity, on intentions, on faith; then again

Intentions or faith alone would not suffice to lead one on a straight path, the circle thus closing upon itself, like a serpent attempting to devour its own tail

Ioakim is thinking, being dragged behind his thoughts, stumbling.

But now the fox as well as Andronikos' torture

If he spoke, voiced, verbalized, the thoughts as rapidly as they crossed his mind since the evening, would he come close to what Andronikos had done?

He would not.

Andronikos had been forced to talk for eight straight days.

For eight straight days, more than food or water, he had been forced to swallow air. For eight straight days.

Eight days, eight nights

First he had spoken of God, then of his deeds, then of his beliefs, then of his disbeliefs, then of unbelief, then of the essential precepts in his heart, then of his essential worthlessness, then of his suffering, then of his fatigue, then of friendship, then of love, then of indifference, then of his childhood, then whatever came to his mind or his lips, then, finally, whatever could not even leave his heart or mind.

He had not spoken.

He had been forced to speak.

Then, faster, faster, he had spun like the spinning wheels of a toppled cart. Then the spinning had slowed down, then down, then stopped until it was forced to resume, then it had stopped, then been forced to resume, then, later

The candle had burnt its wick. The wheel had gotten stuck. Later it had squeaked, then

Stopped. Outright. While speaking — screaming — of the vanity of feeling pride for one's mistakes.

For Ioakim, now

Now, in the face of the news secretly brought to him this morning by a young monk who asked to speak in private, making sure no one could overhear them

This is even beyond humility.

A man debased, bloodied, torn to pieces for having committed a crime, for having sought forgiveness, for submitting to his punishment.

At the point where all roads are impassable, all evenings end, all winters begin.

What is a slave's relationship to his master? What he is thinking of is not the slave who is beaten to submission by the evil master, who runs away or rebels, who kills or is killed in the end. For centuries people have thought in this mold. For centuries, since the beginning of humanity, slaves are beaten, worked to exhaustion, or crushed, while the masters beat them, make their slaves fan them or massage their legs swollen from laziness. But would it be wrong to think of a relationship in which the slaves are loyal to their masters out of love, out of genuine affection, while the masters grovel in dirt to win their slaves' love?

What if the slave loves his master so much that he wishes to die by his master's hands? What if the runaway slave returns to his master, begging to die by his hands? What if the master, in killing his slave, displays the highest mark of his servitude to his slave, by fulfilling the ultimate wish of someone who had loved him as no one else could, by giving his slave the most terrifying gift he has asked for? The highest mark of his servitude, consequently, of his love, of his respect?

Would it truly be madness to think this way? Those who have lived through the experience, those who have experienced the feeling, those who have truly been someone's slave or master, would they consider it madness?

Ioakim doesn't think so, not at all.

If a master does not love his slave enough to fulfill his wish to die by his master's hands, would it not be only fitting that he die by his slave's hands? Would it not be just?

Or is it unthinkable that a master would provoke his own murder by refusing the slave what he asks of the master so that the master can ask it for himself?

Tonight, morning seems like it will never arrive. Yet morning will arrive. It has never failed to arrive. On this night journey, Ioakim must not turn back, even if he's exhausted

Heroism, perhaps

Why be afraid? Perhaps heroism means accepting enslavement, does it not?

As if these thoughts are as much his as they are not.

As if he had read them somewhere, or heard someone else voice them.

But this someone else, whether it was Jesus or Andronikos, whether he voiced or thought them before him, these thoughts are not at all foreign to Ioakim. As if he had thought them himself, a long time ago. It no longer matters. Which thought only belongs to us? If someone says something before we do, can we assume that he had not benefitted from someone else's wisdom? How can we? How can we assume such a thing?

Does heroism not mean accepting enslavement? At least in one sense? Accepting enslavement to such an extent, internalizing it so much, assimilating it so deeply that rebellion — the first act of heroism — can bring about the hero's death at the hands of the one he loves the most, the one who therefore enrages him the most, the one through whom he can experience annihilation?

As for rebellion, does it not necessitate that one must first internalize something, take it seriously, commit to it, feel the weight of that commitment?

Viewed in this manner, too, what Andronikos had done was heroic.

His small habits — the reasons for his rebellion — were themselves the requisites of some form of slavery. They were slavery itself.

Words, too. Words uttered, more so, words given, promises, could they not be perceived as the concretion of one's enslavement? Becoming a hero in the name of one form of slavery, against another form of slavery; turning to the same master, asking him, *kill me, take me in, annihilate me*

A wheel is spinning in the emptiness, Ioakim stands on the hub of this wheel

Ioakim still does not wish to be a hero.

Annihilation, then. That's what Andronikos had asked for. Ioakim wished to stand on the other side of heroism, to be left behind. He did not scrutinize too much the subject of faith; choosing happiness, the last path available

Happiness

This is not exactly a new thought; how many years had passed since he first thought that choosing happiness would be the last path available?

Since he hadn't chosen happiness, hadn't even considered choosing it, no paths had remained for him.

Therefore he had escaped.

He could have escaped to an island, to *the island*, or to Cappadocia. By defying the edict, by rejecting it, he would have become a traitor; by joining the dissenters, he would have become a hero. But by escaping to Ravenna

As if he knew from the start that he would not have stayed in Ravenna. Going there to renew the old belief was an excuse he could offer those who asked why he had left. But by escaping to Rome, by seeking refuge in the Bishop of Rome, he would have been cursed, reviled by everyone, whether in Byzantium or in the fugitives' valley. He would have forfeited heroism altogether. He would have neither returned to his master nor joined the runaways who had rejected their masters. He would have become neither slave nor hero. Nobody would have forced him to speak. He would have remained silent. Truly.

Andronikos had learned absolute silence on the Island; by returning from the Island, he had succeeded in expressing the absolute. If someone asked Ioakim to say a few words at a gathering where everyone spoke, or to sing when everyone sang, he felt something terribly degrading about speaking or singing.

But was it always so?

This no longer matters either.

Ioakim would choose another master.

Become a slave who changed masters as his heart desired.

But once he changed masters, he would also cease to be a slave. Slaves did not choose their own master. Coercion was essential to enslavement.

Ravenna . . . did it ever amount to anything other than a lame, pitiful excuse?

Rome greeted the Emperor's envoys in Ravenna as if they were the Emperor himself. In Ravenna, it was impossible to free oneself from the master. Trying to stay in Ravenna would have been the worst lie one could tell oneself. Lying is a condition of slavery, but lying cannot tolerate cheating. To begin telling the truth while lying was as much cheating as lying while telling the truth.

He had tried to steer clear of it.

Just last year, when the Frankish king arrived in Rome, his reception had been organized like the reception of the envoys sent to Ravenna. Ioakim had felt an eerie chill at the time. Even after years of thinking that he had his deliverance, he was still hounded by the Emperor. As it turned out, Rome had changed masters on that day. Since then, something had been changing in Byzantium, too.

This morning, what the young monk said

He had quickly tried to steer clear of lying. He acknowledges it now. More clearly than he had at the time. . . . He had traveled down to Rome to steer clear of lying. Down to the edge of the swamps near Rome.

What he had done was something akin to asking his enemy for sanctuary just so he could persist in his enmity. He had indeed been granted sanctuary.

When asking the Bishop of Rome for a place to keep the old faith alive, Ioakim had been particularly careful to behave within the confines of faith. A bit like the dying patient who asks for his hair to be combed.

He understood his behavior now. That is, he was able

to interpret it. "Now" is just a few hours ago — which already feels as remote as a few months, a few years ago. ... Because now he has arrived somewhere altogether different.

In reality, he had been trapped in a deep swamp, unaware that he was sinking as he struggled to escape. Now, in light of this morning's news, the church he had built, the church adorned with icons, the shrine he had erected while appearing to struggle to preserve the faith of his homeland, is rendered entirely superfluous.

Thirty-five years

Has it been thirty-five, or less, or more? He seems to have lost count, but does it even matter? When the icons were permitted again

At first the people around him had called it a trick, a plot, refusing to believe, claiming that the palace wanted to identify those who welcomed the dispensation so they could be rounded up, thrown in the dungeon.

As for him, after spending thirteen or fourteen years without icons, Ioakim had neither felt particularly happy that the icons had returned nor harbored suspicions like the others. For a short while, he had wondered whether Andronikos' death had been in vain, whether Andronikos' suffering, the suffering of so many others, had made a difference, but later he had changed his mind. Thinking in this vein would all the more degrade their legacy.

Because the return of the icons had changed nothing.

Nothing had stirred inside him. The resident monks had not experienced oppression in the least, behaving as they always had. Other monks had arrived, seeking sanctuary in his monastery. Because no one disturbed the scribes' monastery.

The prohibition of icons had not spelled the end of the Empire. He wondered whether the world had seemed different to those who had refused to — or couldn't — abandon icons, those who had retreated to the scribes' monastery to carry out their faith in the secret manner that everyone knew all too well.

Now he

Finds himself in a degrading situation, caught in a degrading act, the degradation of escape

Or is he trying to exonerate himself by thinking so?

Though within a year, when another ruler from the old East — not the new East — rose to the throne

How strange that he still thinks in these terms. Here, in the West, after all these years, still perceiving the Eastern rulers of his homeland as aliens. . . . Yet

With the old Easterner on the throne, the dreadful oppression had started. The monks who had retreated to Ioakim's monastery had begun fleeing to more remote monasteries. Soon, the resident monks, too, had followed suit, proving with their actions that they were the most unrepentant iconophiles, willing to do everything to provoke a merciless battle against themselves.

After, long after his escape, Ioakim had continued to receive terrible news. . . . New laws, new edicts were being passed. Monasteries were forbidden to accept novices, training of monks was prohibited.

Later, the monks were ordered to renounce their vows, to evacuate the monasteries, to return to secular life.

As the news arrived, those around Ioakim had praised, venerated him for having foreseen the events, for braving myriad tribulations in strange lands to safeguard the old faith, to preserve the monk's way of life. A hero, they were calling him. Hearing the word would only compound his torment, causing him to feel all the more acutely the new form of enslavement this new path had brought about, this new path that he had taken with his own feet.

If he told them how he had drowned a sick, helpless kit fox, they would still praise him, blaming his deed on his youth or his grief.

Evidently, he had had to wait for this morning to come, to free himself of this heroism that even absolves one of sins or malice.

Now, while everyone, even the doorman, sleeps, in this hour when the monk who brought news from his homeland — the youthful, slender monk with the bashful yet fiery gaze — appears perfectly still, as if in death's sleep behind the slightly open curtains, in the adjacent cell assigned to him by Ioakim on the pretext that the tired messenger must not be disturbed, in this hour when everyone else sleeps the fearless, peaceful sleep of a flock shepherded by a hero, Ioakim feels, lives, perhaps the greatest joy of his life alongside its greatest sorrow.

Until this morning, Ioakim had known what he was not, only what he was not, according to the precepts of religious dogma, of monastic life.

Now, in this moment when he gazes at the yawning emptiness of the palace interiors before him, when he watches the sea, burning in brilliance, about to fill this emptiness with its three arms — how his eyes can still behold these vivid scenes, these images —

He finally know what he is
that he is
defeated, therefore
victorious.
He knows.

The reality of the moment may change again. But he will not have to account for it again. Ioakim knows it.

On the hill, the time when he turned his back on the sunset, on the other hill, when the sun was setting to his left, he now knows what he had been looking for.

As someone unfamiliar with hunger, who had not sought the pleasure of satisfying any form of hunger, who hadn't even allowed such a thought to cross his mind, he had sought to attain his life's essence, to construe an explanation for this existence, to lend it a meaning. It's done now. . . . He found the meaning.

Somehow or other, one is able to live with certain fictions, he says to himself. In my youth, had I embraced fictions more, escaped into them more, heroism

Had I accepted heroism, probably I would not have been able to reach this point today. A step beyond the perfect fiction lies death, he says, I know but now I can, without deceiving myself or turning a blind eye, die inside this edifice, this hollow, boundless fiction, as if the fruit that I carried, toiled all my life to see ripen to perfection, was the same perfect fruit that I conjured in my mind's eye while climbing up the hill this evening.

From here on, the sun will be able to rise to his right
But he will not return to his homeland
He will face the sunrise
If he ever climbs the hill.
He does not think he'll climb again.

From here the path of descent begins. He'll walk down this path, carrying on with his small habits.

He won't struggle to rid himself of these habits any longer; all manner of confrontation, resistance, will lose its meaning along this path that descends straight to death. The westward path.

Descending toward the river that runs through the fallen walls — rain-muddled currents carrying baskets, dog carcasses to the narrowest of the sea's three arms — the path that will come to an end, perhaps just past the mouth of the giant sewer.

This is the victory in defeat; it will bear not the slightest trace of heroism.

In the morning, he should greet his flock in ceremonial vestments.

Maybe he should tell them something like this, as if

recounting a tale: Once upon a time, a man saddled with everyone's sorrows....

This man's greatest sorrow was that he never got to experience his own life or to drown himself in his own sorrows, his own joys, because he always rushed to others in need, sharing in their troubles, their sorrows. He provided for those who looked to him for their livelihood, offered happiness to those who looked to him for their happiness. He was exhausted. Every time his heart rose in revolt against his predicament, he decided to be selfish but in no time found himself answering someone else's call for help, replying, "Here I am." Endlessly vacillating, he came to lie down on his death bed when, suddenly, he saw it in its striking clarity: His own life had been nothing other than this "Here I am." Nothing. He wanted to live by "Here I am"; so he did.

He should tell them something to this effect.

But then he must immediately utter something that would seem to invalidate this story.

He should say, I didn't leave Byzantium because I saw nothing that could be done there; rather, I escaped because I did not want to do anything.

Then, he should say the one thing that will entirely confound them:

My children, I came before you in my ceremonial vestments because we must perform a funeral. Actually, two funerals. That of my life with that of yours.

Starting today, you can live under this roof as subjects of a different creed. Even though the Archbishop has exerted no pressure on the matter — neither do I expect such pressure — I will unite this church with the church of Rome, then retreat to my cell to await my death. Those who do not wish to accept can return either to Ravenna or to Great Constantine's capital.

They can return because

Ioakim doesn't need to sermonize or to rehearse the sermon to himself. They can return because this was the news the young monk brought this morning.

Ioakim will not climb the hill again. He is certain.

According to the young monk, the new Emperor was relaxing the old laws; in the first opportune moment, he was determined to revoke the laws altogether. Those who had heard the Emperor say so had spread his words throughout the city.

The book is finished. The shutters are drawn. Peace is made.

Without fame, without honor.

One evening on a shore in Thessaloniki, he had gazed at the sea, past the sails, at the deep sea, for several minutes that had seemed to last for hours. He recalls watching the slow descent of darkness on the purple sky following the sunset, on that most beautiful shade of purple in the world, the Tyrian purple of the emperors' birthing room, the purple of porphyry, the purple the travelers describe having seen on the rock faces of Eastern mountains. The last color of the night outside his window.

The first color of this morning.

I'm tired, Ioakim thinks. Tired. Is God not going to take my life?

1964–65

THE MULBERRY TREES

Translated by Fred Stark

THE MULBERRY TREES

I can't believe my eyes. The mulberry trees are in leaf again, their branches green.

I got up from the piano that day, went to the kitchen and sliced some bread, which I arranged on a plate and brought to the table. Then I sat down again to do thumb exercises for a few minutes. Mother called me to the table. We sat down. I reached out and took the top slice of bread. Exposed suddenly, the scorpion arched its tail. Mother, who had just taken her first bite, nearly choked on it.

She had gotten up from the piano in a flurry that day, when my father came in carrying his newspaper. "Mi fa proprio impazzire, oggi." Plainly enough, *I* was driving her crazy. Yet I had felt the moment she walked through our door that something else had made her mad even earlier. The lesson was at an end. When my father came in carrying his newspaper, she complained bitterly of my laziness, but went on without giving him a chance to reply. "Imagini pure, signor Karasu, quelle scorpionaccio, quelle scorpionista." I knew that scorpionaccio was what she called Mussolini, but I had never heard scorpionista before. She was explaining heatedly to my father how they had ordered her down to the consulate. Having been forgotten, I too got up from the piano.

It's scarcely believable. The mulberry trees are leafy again, this June of 1960, their branches green. Only a month ago — not even a month — it had taken just days, just a few hours you could almost count, for those beautiful rich leaves to turn, right before our eyes, into the gooey spit of caterpillars. I turn down the road now, walking without revulsion beneath the trees. The layered leaves must be barring the June heat. Underneath them it's cool, the grass at the base of the trees is fresh and straight.

Closing the lid of the piano quietly, I had slid down off the three cushions — the keyboard came to my chest when I sat, the stool wouldn't turn, or perhaps its threads were worn smooth, I can't tell — trying not to let them fall. I had carefully set the cushions back in their places on the Damascus settee, gone over and stood by the open window. There was a door, one-third blocked off by the gilt frame of the ceiling-high console mirror and by the end of a marble slab on which stood tall, pink-globed lamps that I had never seen lit — I had always wondered how they might be — and the obstructing of this door — I had never seen it opened — was made complete by the couch pushed up against it on the other side. From that side now came a voice. "Good for you," it said, "you've practiced hard today. Now go and rest." Then the cat came up behind me, jumped onto the sill, rubbed herself against the wall, paced back and forth a time or two and settled in front of me. Sitting on her haunches, she began rubbing her nose against my chin. I stroked and petted her, then stretched my hand out for the Domenica del Corriere, folded double on the couch, which had been bought from the next-door news stand for me to take home. I reached over the cat's back to prop the magazine against the sill, and turned the light blue cover.

I must be confusing things. My hand goes to the tree trunk — smooth and clean. I look up. Not one thread, not one strand, not a single caterpillar hanging from its line of goo. I must be confusing things. If I had been sent for piano practice to "auntie's" house because my grandmother was dying, then it ought to have been a May morning in 1938. But in that case I really should have been at school. If it was before I went to school, that takes us back to 1936, when I couldn't possibly have practiced the piano without someone helping. And anyway I had started lessons in October, not before. It would have been out of the question in 1936 for a May magazine to show a smoking, dusty, thick-browed, great-eyed, bloody-bandaged smiling picture from a glorious battle won by the united troops of Franco and Mussolini, all of them tassel-capped. Does my recalling all this mean I read the caption? If I did read it, if I could understand that much Italian, then it must have been 1937 at the earliest, even though I knew the alphabet and could read individual words by 1935. And by 1937 I had begun school, so we come back to the same problem. But if my grandmother was dying it had to be May 1938. Let's say it happened in May, that I was going to school but there was some vacation or other.

After perusing thoroughly the first page, with my chin resting on the cat's back, I turned as always to the last page, where there was a color picture in every issue. This time it showed bare-foot, bare-headed, black-skinned men, their eyes bulging with fear, waving their spears or their empty hands as they fled toward the right of the picture. Behind them came some things I knew were called tanks, and there were airplanes circling overhead, while on all sides one saw explosions, burstings of flame, dust and smoke. Behind the black-skins ran some men in tasseled caps and feathered hats, carrying rifles with knives attached. It must have been later that I learned those men in feathered hats were called "bersaglieri," and that you did not say knife but bayonet when it was attached to a rifle. But one thing was plain from the picture. Those tasseled and feathered men, the bayonets, the flames on the ground and the flame in the sky, were all there to kill the blacks. The job at hand was to kill the blacks. Did I make out "Italians" and "Ethiopians" from the caption, or was it because I knew already that Italians in a place called Ethiopia in Africa — the Africa of cannibals — but no, that came later, the day some strange noises rose from the street and I ran to my father and asked him, and when he told me yes I said, then the cannibals are coming, that day must have been some time afterwards, when I had learned how cannibals yell from the Tarzan movies. Anyway, it may have been that I could understand the picture because I already knew that in a place called Ethiopia, in Africa, Italians were killing people for the fun of it. I'm not sure. If it's so, then May 1936 is the time, but I must be confusing things, superimposing images. As far as the post office door there is not a single thread, not one caterpillar swinging; not one trace on the road or among the grass of the month-ago slaughter of leaves. During those days, take all the care I might, still when I reached the post office door I would have three or four of them — in my hair, on my back, neck, chest, pant-legs, sleeves — to pick off with a disgust left from childhood and throw to the ground. The ones my feet squashed on the way made a softer sound. These that I plucked off my hair and clothing, perhaps because I crushed them on the pavement, sounded crisper.

I got up from the table, and after opening the stove door grabbed the tongs. The scorpion on the bread plate was still arched to kill, tail in the air. Cautiously I seized it in the tongs and passed it through the open door onto the glowing coals. It still hadn't stung itself as I closed the door, but then I thought I heard a bubbling. Then popping, as of corn or chestnuts. Mother snatched up the bread plate and took it to the kitchen. We sliced a fresh plateful.

The leaves had melted away in two or three days. Just like the mulberry leaves in my silkworm box, when the worms would reach the size of a finger. The greengrocer used to bring leaves every morning, and they would be munched away in neat paths. For minutes on end I would stand by the box and listen to the rustling worms eat. But those days, no rustling came from the trees. Not that these caterpillars ate silently, but because those soldiers of another May, waiting with rifles stacked, were laughing and talking, very softly, but still, louder than the caterpillars. A mile or more off in the square they were milling, singing, being chased, running, absorbing blows, being arrested, not fearing, singing, milling together, marching; but here it was soldiers smoking, their rifles stacked, laughing and talking softly. The caterpillars gnawed at their leaves, hanging full and plump on the strands of goo they dropped. Letters were arriving late, foreign papers and magazines not at all. In a few days, not one leaf would remain in the whole grove of trees.

While now, the sun can't even get through the leaves.

With a month's interval, the trees are leafing again a second time. Twice in one year, twice in one month. Feeling that the caterpillars have all been destroyed, they are sprouting, in the reek of fuel oil, once again.

"Twice in one month," she had told us one day — I was grown up now, she had said, and could hear such things — "Twice in one month they chased us through the streets with clubs. Once when we were leaving the theater, once after a movie." Back when I was first taking lessons from her she had told my parents her story, full of things I didn't understand, and had taken his picture out to show them. Naturally I had looked too. He was terribly handsome. As she held out the picture to me — had I been older I no doubt would have realized how proud she felt — she had said once again, "This is my husband." His eyes were so light as to be indiscernible in the brown, chiaroscuro picture. I asked, and she told me they were a very light blue. His nose sloped beautifully, and turned up slightly in a sharp tip. His thick lower lip delineated a sulk. The picture was in profile, the man gazing absently toward my left shoulder. The thick lower lip was curled in perhaps a smile. His hair must have been quite fair. Giving back the picture I had asked his name. "Gigi," she had told me. "Where is he?" I asked.

"Very far away. In Argentina."

Somehow I had sensed that asking why would be in poor taste, and had kept quiet. The story which at that time she had told only to my parents I too learned, but later, in bits and pieces, according to the mood of certain days, depending on how much she felt like telling. And what she told did not make Gigi shine. Yet underneath her seeming denigration of him lay a longing. I think I can say that now with perfect certainty.

A month ago I would never have believed that a tree — any tree — could put forth leaves twice in one year. One year? Twice in one month. But now I can say it with perfect certainty. I have seen it in my own lifetime. In order to survive, the trees did what that summer required, in spite of the caterpillars. But there is still a question. Will they be able, now that their berries have fallen, been crushed, will they be able to bear them again? For this year, at least, the trees have no need of berries. But will they make that effort too? My hand is on the trunk, stroking it. I see it clean and smooth; like the leaves.

"Are you Catholic?"

"Yes."

"How can you prove it?"

"What do you mean?"

"Do something to make us believe it."

"Just where in God's name do you think we are? This is a consulate, not a church. And you're not a priest. What's more, this is one subject no one can...."

"Listen, madam, this isn't easy for me to begin with. You're acquainted with Father M...."

"No, I'm not acquainted with him. I'd simply heard he would be coming. To replace Father S., who we've heard had some trouble here. Who they say was sent to Sardinia when he couldn't say the right words or make the right sermons. I was going to have seen Father M. for the first time next Sunday. And you're quite aware that I couldn't know him."

"That's true, you couldn't know him. Yes. And of course I've known you for some years. But you see, we've received this new directive...."

"And now maybe you'll ask me whether I go to confession. But the trouble is, *you see*, that...."

"Please don't get upset, madam, please."

"That's when I blew up. Right there in front of his desk I went through the whole Credo. Does that suit you, I said. And what does he do but tell me to cross myself."

My father had looked sardonic. "That's how far they've taken things now. What can you say?"

"What can you *say*? But I'm not finished. Listen to what comes next. Very well, he said, you're Catholic, I've often seen you in church. What about your mother, though? Was she Jewish? And I had thought he'd be too embarrassed to say any more. What's that supposed to mean, I said. Well, he said, her name was Rachele, wasn't it? I looked him straight in the eye. Il signor Mussolini, I said — you should have seen their faces when I didn't say il Duce, they went green — il signor Mussolini had a Donna Rachele in his family, if I'm not mistaken. She wouldn't be Jewish, would she? They changed the subject right away. The one they called a priest left the room, and that German-looking woman, with the man from the embassy, went over toward the window.

"You're married, is that correct?"

"Yes."

"But your husband is not in Turkey."

"No. He's in Argentina, in Buenos Aires. At least that's where he was when I last heard from him."

"Don't you hear from him?"

"I haven't for approximately ten years."

"Is he alive then?"

"How should I know?"

"Have you tried at all to get word of him? Haven't you done anything?"

"I have, I've tried. But nothing came of it."

"All right then, madam, thank you. You've been very patient."

"Proprio cosi, signor Karasu, proprio cosi. It's incredible, it's simply awful."

She had paused. "They were after something, but I couldn't tell what. Perhaps they didn't know themselves, and were only groping. The things they ask were so unrelated. If Gigi's dead — it's possible. Suppose they know he's dead. That would make all those questions pointless. Of course, he isn't dead. Then what put it into them to . . . interrogate me that way? I haven't heard of them calling anyone else in. Well, suppose they just happened to start with me, it's still funny. They must know I don't have the slightest interest in politics. My pupils and their families, my old friends — those are the only people I see. Surely they're aware of that. I'm sick most of the time anyway, with one thing or another. Who knows, maybe the Germans put them up to it. They thanked me and sent me away. I still don't understand. Isn't it just incredible?"

"It is," said my father. "Incredible."

I smiled. "All right, signora Pozzi, let's do something else incredible. Play that Giovinezza for us."

She looked at me crossly, then laughed. "Why not? It's a good song, I like it. Why shouldn't I play it? Just because it's sung by the Fascists."

She sat down to the piano again. I stood behind her. "Giovinezza . . . . Di bellezza. . . . . . ." It was clear that singing this song which began with "youth," she was recalling her own, and Gigi. The bond between the Mussolini youth song and the shattering of her own happiness was, for the moment, forgotten. Gigi, whom she had loved madly, with whom she had more or less eloped, was now far away. Her voice rose, grew richer, then softened again at the point where it would surely have cracked. This woman, who had fled from Mussolini's gangs, from the beatings, from the attacks, to Turkey, here in Turkey sat singing Giovinezza. And wasn't that incredible?

Like these leaves. These leaves I see before me.

About two hours after they played Giovinezza, the radio upstairs tuned in on London would be sending down Lili Marlene, husky, slow, full of pain, in the peaceful blacked-out night. Downstairs, the radio tuned in on Berlin would be sending up Lili Marlene, husky, slow, full of pain. This song, though at the time I did not realize it, would for certain people, myself above all, bring surging up in the heart — our hearts — a host of longings, sorrows, memories. The song of Lale Anderson. At that time I did not realize how, in those pitch-black blacked-out nights, we all were unafraid.

At first I did not realize, that day. I had turned up the road, eyes downward, going toward the post office. There was a rustling off to my right and I looked over. Three soldiers were squatting on the ground. I went on, then stopped. What were soldiers doing here? Squatting by threes and fives under the trees, smoking, whispering. Laughing now and then. Their voices would rise a tone, then go back to a whisper. Their weapons were stacked in front of them. They must have been moved in here under the trees in case the people singing in the square a mile off came up this way. What difference would it make if they did come? They were singing down there, marching arm in arm, not breaking or damaging anything. If they came up here they'd no doubt be told to stop. And if they didn't stop, what then? Would the soldiers get the order to open fire? Near the end of April they had opened fire in Ankara, then Istanbul, one day apart. The anger had swollen. There was still marching, there was still singing. Shooting would be just as unthinkable, now, as it would be hideous. Anyway, there was no one coming up here. The songs, the beatings, the scatterings, chasing, shouts, all stopped a half mile away. Going into the post office I suddenly shuddered with revulsion. Up my sleeve was crawling a green, husky caterpillar. My hand at the nape of my neck took hold of an even fatter, greener one, and threw it to the floor. I shook myself all over, the way a cat or dog shakes itself. The clerks in the post office looked at me half-mockingly, but smiling, as if to say the same thing had happened to them. There was a girl, maybe seventeen or eighteen years old, who reached her hand out to my back, then brought it away. With the tip of her shoe she squashed one more caterpillar. My whole body was seized with an itching, as it had been in 1943 during the typhus epidemic. When I left the post office and went outside I saw them, each on its thread, swinging. Most of them were still high up, no more than two or three had dropped to head level. In the days that followed they would all grow larger, and hang lower. To make that walk, you would all but have to carry an umbrella with you. In the square a mile away, the number of arrests was increasing.

There had been only one kind of newspaper, one kind of labor union, able to survive. The parties had not been shut down yet, but it was obvious they soon would be. People spoke in whispers and in private: What should be done, what can be done? Gigi had at one time gone up to France, but instead of collecting his wife had hastily returned home. Two days later a law was passed depriving of their rights of citizenship all those who had opposed the regime and were abroad. I didn't want to be left without a country, he told Giulia. And she did not ask him how he had known the law would be passed. Every day word reached them of friends beaten up, forced into alleys on the way home at night and clubbed; or else, at pistol point, threatened with clubbing, made to drink whole bottles of castor oil. Some of them had died, others been crippled. One night as they had just left the theater they realized that some people were following them. Gigi had said to walk a little faster, but not to make it obvious; maybe they could find some doorway to hide in. They were scared. They had walked clear to the end of the boulevard, thinking they might not be assaulted under all those lights. The men had kept following. Finally there was nothing for them to do but turn into the side streets, into a steadily deepening darkness. There wasn't a car in sight. And if there had been, how much good could it have done? At the first corner they turned Gigi had taken Giulia by the hand, and they ran like crazy. She took off her shoes to run more freely, though the pavement hurt her feet. But she was afraid, terribly afraid, of those men behind her. Left, right, they kept turning as they ran. They were exhausted, but they ran. All the doors were shut tight, in the great palazzos and the small houses. Sometimes they would hear nothing, but then as they turned a corner the sound of running feet would fill their ears again. Whoever it was hadn't given up. Gigi was from Florence, but he knew this part of Rome like a native. Giulia was beside herself at any rate, following wherever he led. "Thank God my skirt was a short one. I happened to be following the fashion. I never would have dared to do such a thing in Florence." They were still running. Giulia had been slender in those days, but still the running was too much for her, she had no breath left. "Gigi just dragged me along." Suddenly there had been a door ajar beside them, a narrow door. They hurled themselves inside, gasping, and made to push it shut. "You think I left it open for you, huh?" The voice was low, husky, cracked. Gigi embraced Giulia, kissed her for a long time to cover up their panting. "This may be the right place," came the voice, "but we don't rent it to strangers." The sound of running and hoarse shouts drew near, and they could hear swearing. After a while it moved away. "All right, clear out of here." The voice in the darkness sounded weary. "I don't want trouble all over again." They left — they had to — without the least glance into the dark where the woman's face was. Clinging to the walls, they began their walk home. They had gone ten paces when they heard a door shut behind them. Footsteps were coming up behind, closer, closer. The man who passed them, with his fur-collared coat, silver-engraved cane and derby hat, with his brisk important strides that soon faded in the distance, would later afford them a hearty laugh whenever they remembered that night. But not that night. The walk took twenty minutes, and every street corner had made them choke with fear. "The second time, twenty-four days later, we were leaving a movie." It had been raining, and she had her umbrella. Gigi carried a steel-tipped cane, and a gun in his pocket. They were still afraid nights, but now at least they were prepared. They had been attacked once, and the world had changed for them. "This time there was a fight. We weren't alone, Gigi's brother was with us. Pint-size, just a boy, but for three weeks he'd been carrying a jack-knife. Anyone who goes after my brother goes after me, he'd say. I'd gotten my back to a doorway, and there I was, jabbing right and left with that umbrella as though it were a spear. *And* I was screaming, till my lungs turned inside out. No one came to help, of course, but you can be sure they heard me. Everyone on that street must have been watching us from behind their shutters. Maybe they had watched other people that way, other nights. Maybe there came a night when other people watched them. Anyway, I imagine we batted those thugs around pretty well, even wounded them. But Gigi and his brother were all bruised, all cut up, their clothes torn everywhere. They both had split eyebrows. I'll bet some blood flowed on the other side too, that knife wasn't there for nothing. But the gun stayed put away, thank God. The others hadn't drawn their knives. That's right, it's funny. They just used the clubs. Then suddenly they stopped fighting and left in a gang. "Let that be a lesson to you," they shouted. If you ask me they were scared of the knife. Anyhow, we got home that night too, bloody as we were. I never went out again though, not after dark. Gigi only left me alone at night when he had meetings. And in any case, we left before long for Istanbul."

Istanbul hadn't suited him. Giulia had begun to find some lessons and was earning a living. When the steamer

Gigi worked on came back to Istanbul, it carried a letter saying that he had found a job in Buenos Aires and would stay there. Three years later he had come back, and weeping begged her to be patient another year. But Giulia was through with moving on. "He was handsome, brave, cheerful, full of humor; but how could he have fought Mussolini's gang from half a world away? Wasn't he bright enough to see that? I wonder."

Or were these men, I wonder, borne by their mothers to be battered? Were these children brought to the world to die, to be shot? As the people marching and singing swelled in number, the people who published by the grapevine the whole news of the day, the people the cops were chasing, working over, arresting, taking away; as they swelled in number, and the stories took shape which today fill every column of every magazine and paper in the land; while all this grew, there were certain men turning blinder by the hour. And the caterpillars, having stripped clean their trees, hung from the stark branches of that late spring, always nearer to the ground. A few weeks later the pumps were brought in. I went up to the post office that evening holding my nose, with one hand slapped over my mouth. That day there were no more soldiers. I thought, there's still someone who cares about these trees. But fuel oil might not do the job. If they held a match to them. . . .

But no fire was needed for the cleanup. Maybe that's for the best, maybe not. Afterwards it rained, for hours, pouring down in a flood from the sky. The trees stood in a lake. There were more songs. Those songs will bring back memories, those songs that gave an answer to the others, which had thought a giant river could halt, that the Danube might cease to flow. Those songs of victory.

I take my hand away from the tree. Once again, I look up at the leaves. To believe it. It has to be believed. There they are, holding the sun away. And OF COURSE the Danube flows.

The post office door, at the end of its tree-lined road, draws near.

9 780872 865914